Praise for *On Coventry*

"The protagonist of Matt Schultz's fine debut novel, *On Coventry*, is Eliot Hopkins, a deeply introspective, passionate young man 'on the tragic side of twenty two,' haunted by his mother's death, his own family's troubled lineage, and wonder struck by new love. *On Coventry* is both a tender Bildungsroman and a sweet Valentine to that great, faded beauty of a city, Cleveland, told in a generous and muscular prose we haven't seen since Raymond Carver ran off with all the adjectives."

–George Bilgere, author of *The Good Kiss*

"Literary fiction with the ink of a gorgeously patterned history tattooed deep into its skin."

–Amitava Kumar, author of
Nobody Does the Right Thing

"Matthew Schultz's *On Coventry* is a love letter to a city, its history and its inhabitants. Each page resonates with the idea 'that the story of our individual and collective histories still lives in each of us.' Each sentence pays moving and lyrical homage to the sense of possibility in every person and place, and every story."

–Dave Lucas, author of *Weather*

ON COVENTRY: A NOVEL

by Matthew Schultz

New York
Harvard Square Editions
www.harvardsquareeditions.org
2015

On Coventry, copyright © 2015 by Matthew Schultz

ISBN 978-1-941861-09-7

Photo © Bradley Schultz

Published in the United States by
Harvard Square Editions

www.HarvardSquareEditions.org

For Arthur,

My beamish boy

"To send one to Coventry; a punishment inflicted by officers of the army on such of their brethren as are testy, or have been guilty of improper behaviour, not worthy the cognizance of a court martial. The person sent to Coventry is considered as absent; no one must speak to or answer any question he asks, except relative to duty, under penalty of being also sent to the same place. On a proper submission, the penitent is recalled, and welcomed by the mess, as just returned from a journey to Coventry."

— *A Classical Dictionary of the Vulgar Tongue* (1785), Francis Grose

October

Inauguration
October 4, 2013

ELIOT HOPKINS sat huddled against the driver's-side window of a pale blue pickup truck chewing the wax from the paper rim of a coffee cup. He breathed deep as if to drink the vapors through his aquiline nose and then mouthed, almost silently, the novel he held open against the crook of his bent knee. A squalid autumnal rain smeared the truck's hazy glass, muting the otherwise brilliant boughs of a knotted Silver Maple aflame with the smoldering orange of another small death. The foggy hue of a girl in a knee-length pea coat, its collar turned up against the swell of her ale-brown hair, splashed across the quad not unnoticed.

Eliot's eyes followed the girl's familiar figure as his hand dialed the truck's AM radio to within a decibel of mute. The weatherman's hushed voice reported that a cold front had stalled over Northeast Ohio, and that there was every possibility the morning's rain would turn into an early-season snowfall by evening. Eliot hadn't observed the moment at which the truck windows became glazed with fog, a byproduct of his ineffectual attempt to breathe life into the fiction buried in his lap. He stabbed at the heater's dial with the spine of his paperback petitioning the dashboard fans to ward off the encroaching brume. The girl vanished.

Eliot tugged at the clay-caked brim of his Cleveland Indians baseball cap, an embroidered 'C' stitched where Chief Wahoo's magnanimous grin typically shone like the beacon of a north shore lighthouse. The truck's cab was heavy with recycled engine heat and the rot of a banana peel decomposing on the passenger-side floor mat. The smell was almost comforting on such a cool, wet day. Reaching down to crack his toes, Eliot allowed himself to sigh his disappointment at the news of a premature snowfall. He tried to recall the bake of August and his initial encounter with the girl who had more recently splashed across the quad.

She must have just left class that afternoon and was descending the narrow staircase into The Underground for a late lunch when she passed Eliot as he climbed out. The girl unconsciously brushed the wall to avoid touching him, but the folds of her skirt had brushed his hand. She smelled of crushed strawberry Pez candy, and had spoken a sentence to one of her friends, of which he only remembered the word *catharsis*. Eliot was struck dumb with love. That word on her tongue, which Eliot did not then understand, possessed the allure of the sacred. Without a glance she passed him by. Eliot, stalled halfway up the stairs, said nothing. But he did recall Haruki Murakami's description of remorse in "On Seeing the 100% Perfect Girl One Beautiful April Morning." He had read the story four years earlier and it had made him cry; he had loved it for that. He hadn't cried since.

Perhaps it was because of this drought that even now he couldn't think of what he might say to the girl given the opportunity. And if he did know what to say he wondered if he could say it. A new voice on the radio announced that the Indians had slouched into the playoffs as the American League's second Wild Card entry—their first post-season appearance since 2007. Eliot was not optimistic. He peeled the cap from his head, and his black hair bent like wind-flattened meadow grass across his forehead. He combed his fingers through it, settling the hairs back into place as if a pitcher ritualistically preparing for the wind-up, and wondered how he got here.

In another October snowstorm, six years earlier, he and his father had driven to Boston for Game Seven of the American League Championship Series, certain the Indians (up three-games-to-one) couldn't drop three in a row to lose the series, and wanting to be in attendance for something special. The Red Sox dealt the Tribe a heartbreaking 11–2 loss. It was not the first disappointment of Eliot Hopkins's brief sixteen years of life, nor the most tragic. Hurling westward on the Massachusetts Turnpike (somewhere between Worchester and Chicopee) and talking of 'next year,' Eliot asked his father, retired Lieutenant Frank Hopkins, to recommend him for a summer job with his pals from the Euclid Fire Department who ran a construction crew on their off days that specialized in updating the wiring of not-quite-dilapidated century homes around Cuyahoga County. Since that winter Eliot had spent his school holidays gutting the remnants of Cleveland's industrial gilded age, while his friends vacationed to places where girls wore less clothing. He rode the scorched vinyl seats of the pale blue pickup through Cleveland's mercurial summers and his late teenage years, envisioning the rank racetracks that littered Charles Bukowski's Los Angeles and the ocean-side rum huts of Hunter Thompson's San Juan. He often imagined what it might be like to spend an afternoon alongside his favorite poets and drunks, islands perched atop ripped leather stools, resting heavy elbows and weary consciences on the bar. His Midwestern sensibilities were enchanted by the gambling and the girls and the booze these men promised resided in faraway lands. His teens became twenties somewhere in between the City of Angels and the rum-soaked island capital.

Now, on the tragic side of twenty-two, a pair of thick black frames dulling an otherwise Kryptonian face that Eliot had been told on multiple occasions resembled Christopher Reeve as Clark Kent, he slouched in the stale cab of an old truck reading, for the third time, a book about false hope. He watched as rainwater flooded into the hole he had just dug in the ground of John Carroll University that would eventually conceal the wiring for a series of Victorian replica sidewalk lamps.

The sluice called to mind a recent late-August weekend spent driving Cornell's tiny, sage-green motorcycle to Red Cloud, Nebraska, while his friends dangerously over-packed their parents' cars and took aim at the Pacific one last time to ponder what one does with a life. The run of water curved around the twisted sidewalk like the motorcycle he had guided around bends in the asphalt. Leaning his brawn into those turns felt more like flying even than soaring through the clouds in an airplane. Eliot still wore the memory of that trip: a farmer's tan earned mile-by-mile upon the Midwest highway flecked with billboards and derelict agricultural equipment. Now, only the backs of his rusted hands betrayed an ongoing struggle with the elements.

The steady plunk of raindrops on the steel roof of the truck became as ferocious and unyielding as the charge of Lord Cardigan's Light Brigade. The thunderous drum rendered the radio completely inaudible. Eliot slurped his coffee. It tasted of blackberry jam and cocoa. He was envious of students' aborted attempts to attend class, surrendering instead to warm, dry covers heaped beneath Elvis Costello posters and surrounded by the refuse of the previous night's festivities. He imagined them slapping at alarm clocks they would later say failed to sound, and, after picking the crust from their eyes to visually confirm the patter of rain on the dormitory's windows, falling back asleep behind the protective bricks of Pacelli Hall. Eliot resented their choices. He felt stuck, like the sodden work boots he lodged between the windshield and dashboard so that they could dry to their original wheat nubuck. At least he could no longer feel the cold stickiness of the rain that had soaked through his tartan flannel shirt as he scrambled from his trench. Eliot Hopkins returned his attention to the Michael Chabon sentence he had been re-reading for the better part of the morning from *The Amazing Adventures of Kavalier and Clay*:

> "The true magic of this broken world lay in the ability of the things it contained to vanish, to become so thoroughly lost, that they might never have existed in the first place."

A mobile phone vibrated upon the truck's dashboard. Eliot pressed the heels of his hands against his eyes, then retrieved a splintered and stained coffee stirrer from behind his right ear and tucked it into the ditch between pages 339 and 340.

"Yeahp?" he asked.

"Pack it in," a voice answered. Eliot peered into the rearview mirror at the driver of the black and chrome pickup truck parked behind him. He stole a brief, worried look into his own blue eyes, inherited from his maternal great-grandfather, before focusing on the reflection of Pat Murphy. Pat, who had always been something of a big brother to Eliot, was promoted to lieutenant when Frank Hopkins retired from fighting fires fourteen years earlier. Pat offered a nod and fanned out his fingers, "We'll give it a go tomorrow."

This narrative had become a well-established pattern in Eliot's life: tomorrow, next year, eventually, somewhen.

"All right," said Eliot, trying to sound disappointed. He pulled his thin lips tight together in something he thought resembled an understated frown. His thumb jabbed a featureless button that extinguished the piss-colored neon of the phone's screen. Pat maneuvered his truck alongside Eliot and they exchanged another quick nod before the pickup set out to navigate the labyrinthine service drives back to the public roads. Eliot continued to wonder at himself in the rearview mirror. Shallow crevices had begun to crease his forehead and the tanned skin around his eyes seemed leathered, cracked. Though he lived his life between the covers of books, a secret admirer of the enchanting, an appreciator of melancholy, Eliot's body had also been molded by the scorching sun and relentless winds that powered through countless construction sites. He enjoyed his status as an adjacent college student, imbibing knowledge at the periphery, unwilling to debauch his reading experience by talking about the fictional lives of others with complete strangers, or, worse yet, mere acquaintances. The real wonder of life, Eliot was certain, occurred in the pollination of a threadbare routine by weighty sentences, the kind he could tuck into the pocket of his mind to more beautifully narrate his seemingly commonplace existence.

Eliot nudged the shifter into first, and, feeling the gnaw of gears engaging through the worn knob beneath his calloused palm, pressed his bare foot to the gas pedal. His toes curled around the side of the thin accelerator. It felt flimsy and small without the wide expanse of a shoe on his foot. He eventually eased the truck to a stop beneath the overhang that protected the East Gate guard shack from the storm, and observed that Pat had already disappeared into the quiet suburb. Eliot waited for the light to change. He was still able to squeeze a few drops from the socks hanging over the heating vents and, judging them uncomfortably wet, yanked his nearly-dry boots over bare feet while his gaze fixed beyond the traffic signal at the twin structures of Campion and Hamlin Halls.

A light flicked on and the girl appeared in a third-floor window. She shook out of the knee-length pea coat and wrung her hair with a towel. A gentle glare of gothic-green glowed through the truck's windshield indicating it was time to go. Eliot disobeyed the signal, intent upon the framed figure across the street. He imagined touching his chapped lips to the lighter-brown strands of gossamer adorning the soft skin of her temple.

"You are un-for-tun-ate," A muffled voice said from outside the driver's-side window. Eliot spun his head in a mix of surprise and embarrassment. The accusation came from within the guard shack. A campus security guard reclined precariously atop a bargain-basement office chair, its back secured by a duct tape tourniquet. He plucked a cigarette from between his lips and looked at Eliot expectantly.

Eliot worked the window crank, lowering the glass just enough to both speak with the man and shelter himself from the blowing rain. Inside the guard shack he spied a series of black-and-white security monitors broadcasting what, today, looked like photographs of the lifeless campus. The Alumni Association could have used any of the scenes as the cover of their annual giving campaign mailer: The American flag obediently sailing between raindrops, a bronzed Saint Ignatius steadfast before the Chapel, the clock tower's unyielding glow. "Huh?" He asked.

The guard, his feet kicked over the corner of a desk, leaned forward the few centimeters he could and repeated his question, "You guys done for the day?"

"Oh," Eliot said. He frowned in the general direction of outside, and rubbed his smooth face as if contemplating a response: "Uh, yeah, we can't really wire anything in this slop."

The guard snorted a burst of air through his nose, slightly jerking the entire upper half of his body, "Fair enough." The light, which had expired during their exchange, once again shone green.

Eliot, eager to be alone, vigorously worked the window crank to once again seal himself in the cab. He managed to slip a "take it easy" through the opening before it shut against the rubber catch.

"You too," The guard said, his attention stolen by the long ash of the cigarette he held between his thumb and index finger. Before pulling away, Eliot watched him cock his digits and flick the entire stub toward an already littered puddle. The filter disappeared beneath the surface. An ashy contrail lingered behind it, and drifted to the ground like snowflakes.

Eliot angled the truck left across a rush of gutter water, the wipers creeping audibly along the windshield. He looked toward the lighted window across the vacant street and found it extinguished, the room's occupant likely lost in the darkness of sleep.

*   *   *

Eliot leaned against the cold steel of the truck, his eyes shut against the station's fluorescent lighting. He watched as a kaleidoscope of shapes and colors played against his eyelids. A few snowflakes stuck in the bush of his eyebrows and melted. The rotary dial on the outmoded gas pump clicked to a stop at $57.94, and Eliot opened his eyes. A block north on East 79th Street Hot Sauce Williams opened their windows to advertise: the smell of barbequed Kielbasa announced that it was lunchtime for anyone in a five-block radius. Eliot could just make out the southeast corner of Lemaud Williams's amaranth pink and Wedgewood blue building, another brilliant stroke of prudent advertising. The stench of gasoline and fried meats, however, did not appeal to Eliot. He wanted to be back in the truck and away from that place as quickly as possible.

From deep within his blue jean pockets Eliot retrieved his hands, and balling them into loose fists against the cold, raised them toward his face to blow hot breath into each like a warrior of ancient India trumpeting a conch shell to announce the War of Kurukshetra. Eliot grasped the nozzle and gave it a rapid squeeze-and-release, persuading six cents worth of gas from the hose. He looked for a slot to insert his credit card, and when one could not be found set out across the cracked and cratered asphalt for the attendant's booth.

Eliot examined the small, white filling station that served as the hub of the Cedar Road and East 79th Street intersection. A tenantless strip mall was decaying on an adjacent corner behind roll-down wire cages that secured the open wounds of wrecked glass windows. Dust from countless shattered beer bottles launched from the nearby bus shelter into the night sky like expectant dreams now glimmered in the parking lot—a million missed opportunities. Brown paper bags beaten into the ground by rain lay motionless like grave markers. Across the street an empty brown dumpster camouflaged in admittedly impressive graffiti sat among a decade's worth of election signs populating an otherwise vacant lot. Only the Dark & Lovely Hair & Beauty Supply shop showed any signs of life: an illuminated marquee, crisply defined parking spaces, a line of red-plastic shopping carts chained to one another outside the door next to a stack of recently delivered newspaper advertisements.

Frustration tugged at Eliot's brow, creasing the skin between his eyes as he got close enough to confirm the unoccupied space behind the glass. No card reader; no attendant. He wanted to be someplace that wasn't this voided intersection. An uncharacteristic impatience stole over him. When he arrived at the barred window, he rapped his chapped knuckles against it, twice. Eliot waited until the attendant appeared from behind a wall of cigarette cartons before sliding his card into the steel tray.

"Pump Four," he said.

"Fifty-eight on the button." The nameplate stitched into the attendant's crisp, white shirt identified the man as 'Vern.' He was small and gray and Eliot envied his solitude. He wondered if Vern was the current proprietor of this depressed Gulf filling station. It looked like a family affair, the whole enterprise having been passed down from father to son when such transactions, he guessed, were still viable. The single garage stall to Eliot's left was cluttered with worn cardboard boxes and rusted aluminum signs and a few dusty vending machines strewn with multi-colored pennant flags that called to mind Memorial Day parades and accompanying root beer barrel candies—his own father's favorite. The jaundiced shell of a '68 Cutlass Supreme perched upon cinder blocks was yet another sign of generational decline advertising a lack of both passion and resource. The thought of the restroom turned Eliot's stomach.

"That all?" Vern asked.

"Yes, thanks," Eliot said.

The shadow of a Greyhound Bus appeared in the glass, stretched thin, and disappeared. Its absence revealed to Eliot an ethereal streak of orange. He turned to note a distended line of construction barrels, and, with his ear now aimed toward the booth, could hear the quick tempo, button-box polka of Frankie Yankovic that Vern was tapping his squat fingers to while he waited for the transaction to be approved.

"Is Cedar down to one lane?" Eliot asked. He jerked his thumb to indicate the direction he was headed toward the electrical company's warehouse downtown. The tone of the question betrayed his frustration. He didn't want to waste the afternoon stuck in traffic when he could be logging hours at the bookstore to make up for the construction wash-out.

Vern tore at the receipt paper streaked with pink dye and pushed it toward Eliot. "Closed, I think. I don't know what the hell they're doing down there."

Eliot heaved a sigh and carved his signature into the paper with the mostly dry pen

"Where you headed?" Vern asked. He licked his index finger to more easily separate the receipt's hidden yellow copy. Eliot's signature hadn't transferred, but Vern passed the receipt to him without concern.

"Euclid and East 30th," Eliot said.

"Mmm." Vern thought a moment, then said through the bulletproof glass, "Just cut up 74th to Central and take 55th to Euclid. Should miss it."

"Thanks," Eliot said, hopeful that he might salvage a few hours worth of pay. "Hey, do you have any of those root beer candies?"

"Uh, like the little barrels," Vern asked, holding up his fingers a half inch apart to indicate what he meant by little.

"Yeah," Eliot said.

"Sorry."

Eliot shrugged indifference and navigated his way between puddles back toward the truck. Climbing in he noticed that Vern had again disappeared behind the wall of cigarettes and chewing gum—the only profitable items peddled at a gas station with no beer cooler. Reaching down with his left hand, Eliot pulled out the choke and, with his right, turned the key. The engine lurched. There followed a few manipulations of the choke, coaxing the engine to settle into a low rumble. Eliot drank in the last sip of his now cold coffee and cradled it in his mouth for a few seconds before dropping the empty paper cup into a holder and putting the truck into gear.

He swung wide out of the Gulf station's parking lot, past the field of expired election signs announcing John C. Dugan's candidacy for Cleveland Comptroller, and out of range of Hot Sauce Williams's aromatic advertising. He detoured south onto East 74th Street.

On the kind of rained-out morning when he would typically retreat to the second floor reading area of Grasselli Library that overlooked the small faculty parking lot (bloated with mid-1980s BMWs and early-1990s Saabs) to read without interruption—except to scan the faces of passers-by, or to eavesdrop on conversations betrayed by the stacks' insufficient insulation, or to peer across the shingles of a dozen Georgian homes, arranged like sentinels to protect the campus from urban blight (a defense he had proved penetrable)—Eliot found himself detoured at the neglected corner of E. 74th Street and Central Avenue, feeling faintly haunted.

* * *

The instant it entered his field of vision, the house felt familiar. It wasn't so much an experience of *déjà vu* as it was a sort of ghostly recognition, which was particularly odd because Eliot had never had the occasion to be at the corner of E. 74th Street and Central Avenue prior to that morning's detour. The house was not unique. Rather, it was almost identical to any of the other homes on the street that were arranged in a tight row typical of post-World War I community planning: three stories of white aluminum siding beneath a peaked roof, an arm's length from its neighbor on either side.

What had really caught Eliot's eye was the 'For Sale' sign, which did not exist in the vague recess of his memory. Aside from the sign, this peculiar house stood apart from the others in only two ways: it sat on a corner lot that contained two crabapple trees, and the awnings that hung above each window were painted a delicious shade of red. The shutters, also red, matched the chipped paint on the three crude stone steps leading to a fully-screened front porch into which Eliot could not see. He squinted and craned his neck. Nothing. His attention was caught by a plastic flag that stood erect, signaling the presence of mail in a white letterbox at the top of the stairs and adjacent to a flameless black gas lamp. Unlike the new fixtures secured in the truck bed, this lamp was worn and half of the decorative ladder rest had broken off. The front yard was comically small—the size you'd likely tend with a manual reel mower, or even an electric weed-wacker.

Binding the yard to the house was a twisted chain link fence. The rusted gate, obviously older than Eliot, hung askew on its hinges, causing it to lean heavily upon the walkway. A small, royal blue aluminum plate was tied to the chain link with a squat metal ring. Its white letters read *Cyclone*, identifying the fence as an antiquated product of the United States Steel Corporation—a company for which Eliot's grandfather, William Hopkins, had worked as a draftsman.

The summer before joining the Euclid Fire Department Frank Hopkins also worked for Cyclone Fence as a field laborer, installing highway guardrail and perimeter fences at maximum-security prisons in Central Ohio. The Cyclone Fence Cleveland Offices closed in 1998, denying Eliot the opportunity to join the ranks of Hopkins men who had stretched wire on the fence line, though his work as an apprentice electrician was not all that different from what his father had done as a post-hole digger. They hated it equally. Frank Hopkins had eventually become a saver of lives. Eliot had yet to prove himself. Eliot's father was his hero. And though he had never conjured the courage to tell him, he hoped that Frank somehow knew. He thought of Vern's Gulf station and the very real phenomenon of generational decline.

Next to the crippled gate sat a large terra cotta planter pot crowned by Quackgrass and Spurge, the same weeds congesting the cracks that fissured the entire cement driveway from the street to the single-car garage. It was not a handsome home, but it possessed a quality that Eliot could not describe, yet drew him in—like the pictures of abandoned steel factories that projected a beautiful sadness: the pornography of decay.

The gutters were overflowing with syrupy bilge. Eliot stared at the house as if seeing it through a veil of memories that were not his own. He looked to the windows for ghosts, a habit he developed as a child after watching a television documentary about hauntings at the Mansfield Reformatory. Since that regrettable night, Eliot stared expectantly into church steeples, hospital rooms, apartment buildings, factories, and ramshackle houses. He was looking for his mother. She had died when he was only a few seconds old. So he studied, both hopeful and not, the dark windows of houses like the one before him, where the play of light on the thin panes of glass shivering against the wind was both perception and hallucination. Neither soul nor body appeared. So, like honey bees beating their wings helplessly against the snow-covered ground, disoriented by the cold, white dust mistaken for sky, Eliot struggled to see more clearly this house that haunted him.

Olivia Hopkins had died from complications that arose during childbirth. As Eliot appeared, she vanished. Her thin fingers, already clammy with perspiration from labor, went limp in Frank's hand and his tears transitioned from merry to grave. In his other hand Frank felt a pair of scissors pressed into his palm by the doctor who asked if he'd like to cut the umbilical cord. The room was silent with the nearly lifeless faces of the medical staff as Frank severed Eliot from his dead mother. Frank's hand grasped tight the shears and slowly cut through the flesh in a moment drawn long like late afternoon shadows. Eliot screamed. At least that is how he imagined his birthday. For something so startling, it seemed incredible how little knowledge he had of this event. Almost everything he knew about his mother—the way she always looked to be dancing in her chair, or how she cupped both hands around a coffee mug to hold in the heat, or even that she seemed always to wear socks that didn't match—he had pieced together by carefully studying old photographs and the too brief inscriptions scratched into their backs. For his twelfth birthday, Eliot had asked his father to tell him a story about his mother. Frank had responded that "she loved life, but it wasn't mutual."

Eliot took a moment to wonder at the chance that had delivered him to this spot, and what it meant to lay his eyes upon the house that he had only ever seen in a single photograph mixed in with pictures of his mother. It had been years since Eliot scraped it from the bottom of the lidless candy tin in his father's kitchen in order to read the back that divulged only, "April, 1922." The leaden apparition of the photographed couple, gathered in each other's arms, began to take shape in the mind's eye of Eliot Hopkins. Their image replaced the black-and-white 'For Sale by Owner' sign currently planted just beyond the crooked fence line. The woman resembled the person Eliot knew as his mother from the old Polaroids. Her arms extended from a bright, sleeveless dress, crumpling her partner's dark suit like the sports section of Monday's *Plain Dealer*. The man was his great-grandfather. He recognized him from another photograph in which he stood against the railing of a sepia-toned ocean liner labeled as the Franz Josef I. That picture was framed and hung in the narrow hallway that led to the bathroom in Eliot's apartment. He waved lovingly goodbye to war-torn Europe and to anyone shuffling toward the Hopkins's toilet. The couple's cheeks and bellies and knees had been captured in an uninterrupted kiss. But their eyes shone apprehensive in front of the haunting house that had, at one time, belonged to Eliot's great-grandparents.

Eliot's mind balked. The faraway mysteries of his mother had begun in this home. He realized in that moment, no longer than the flutter of a camera's shutter, that he would never know his mother's story. Perhaps, though, this house contained within it a smudge of his ancestral past that could make her existence seem a bit more real nonetheless. He had been searching for decades for something outside of himself to reclaim her mark upon the world.

The photographed porch, then screenless, was lined with hanging rhododendrons. A clothesline, strung from tree to tree in the side lot, sagged under the weight of bed linens, trousers, and underpants. There was no Cyclone fence to define their property and no need yet for a garage. The unbroken gas lamp would glisten until 1993. On the porch huddled two rod-iron chairs with green and yellow paisley all-weather cushions. In-between them stood a small, matching table with a frosted glass top that supported a pair of sweating, half-empty glasses of ginger ale. Eliot had once imagined the couple's entire history from the still frame of the warped photograph, but it wasn't until he sat in front of the house that he wondered at the identity of the photographer. That anonymous person had framed for him a fragment of his own history. Eliot had to see for himself what lay at the periphery of the photograph's perception.

He exited the truck, his heart rate increasing with each step closer to the house. Eliot stopped in the spot the camera operator would have stood on that far-gone April afternoon, interrupting his great-grandparents' idleness. He wondered what they spoke about when they were alone, or if they simply proved their love by looking at the same things from a shared vantage point, which was no small matter. It would take a great deal of work to get that close to someone, to see the world through another's eyes as intimately as one accompanies a character in a book. He wondered if he would ever experience such a bond—if he deserved to be loved.

Eliot paused to recall himself half an hour younger, sitting behind the wheel of the pale blue truck, his face blurred by rainwater being swept across the windshield by a mostly inefficient rubber wiper. He tried to imagine how the girl might see him, gazing out from her third-floor window in Campion Hall—his features partially obscured by a baseball cap worn low on his forehead, a frown as slight as the hunch of his shoulders.

Eliot absently walked up the driveway, the heels of his unlaced boots dragging along the uneven concrete, tearing at the Quackgrass and Spurge. Unsure what to expect on this impromptu journey, he flipped the gate's latch and pushed. The sound of cold aluminum squealing against galvanized steel hinges reverberated in his molars and left him marooned at the edge of the yard. Eliot winced at the sight of a figure pushing its way through the frame of the front door and onto the porch. Joseph Kowalski Senior moved deliberately across the threshold, certain to pull shut the wooden door behind him before turning his attention to Eliot, who still stood with his hand upon the gate, only a few steps from the bottom of the chipped red stairs, a mix of rain and snow sticking to his hat and shoulders.

"Hello, there," Joe called warmly and gathered the air before him with a wide swoop that involved both arms as if offering a hug. His voice sounded like the initial wheeze of air rushing from the puncture of an over-inflated balloon. Joe's shoulders were drawn up almost level with his long ears. The acute hunch of his ninety-three-year-old back severely distorted his dimensions. In his younger days Joe had played power forward as a walk on for the Kent State University Golden Flashes. Now, his imperial six-foot-five-inch frame was a crippled five feet, eight inches. With his face angled unhelpfully toward the floor, Joe assessed Eliot's unlaced boots.

"I guess you're ready to take a look inside," he said, smiling. Joe somewhat painfully rolled his eyes toward the crown of his head in order to see if the joke had hit its target.

"Yeah, thanks," Eliot said. He was unsure how long Joe had been watching him. He left the gate ajar to avoid feeling its shriek in the nerves of his teeth. Despite the notion that he was no longer in control of his own circumstance, and that he was being pulled along this walkway by history like a train set upon tracks and hurling through a lightless tunnel, Eliot was agog. He had experienced this feeling before on a few occasions—times when he had found himself in a strange place he would look to someone, perhaps even a complete stranger, to usher him through unscathed. He put his faith in the old man leading him forward. Eliot's eyes widened, his heart beat noticeably, his breath quickened. He climbed the stairs toward Joe who stood at the top wearing a red sweater vest over a navy blue corduroy shirt with mother-of-pearl buttons and grey slacks. His feet looked horrifically swollen until Eliot realized that Joe was wearing two pairs of wool mountaineering socks that added a good half-inch of thickness.

"Joe," said Joe.

"Eliot," said Eliot.

Neither man moved to shake hands. Joe seemed incapable and Eliot disinterested. Not for the last time he questioned his motives for leaving the truck. What had he hoped to gain by steeling a look through the large bay window, now only a few feet away and made obsolete by Joe's invitation to poke around inside? Eliot sighed audibly, which he was not in the habit of doing, and fiddled with one of the buttons on his flannel shirt.

"Looking to move?" Eliot asked.

"Not particularly, but the house is just too damn tall" Joe said. "Trying to climb those stairs is either a comedy or a tragedy. I can't tell anymore."

"Tragedy," Eliot offered.

Joe looked at him, waiting for Eliot to elaborate.

"You're the victim," he connected the dots.

Joe seemed satisfied with Eliot's reasoning. "Anyhow," Joe said, "I'm going to stay with my daughter in Poughkeepsie."

"Where?"

"New York."

"Mmmm," Eliot politely accepted Joe's unhelpful geography lesson. He hadn't heard of Poughkeepsie, and *New York* did nothing to help him locate that peculiar-sounding place. He tried the word out on his tongue, as if hoping to locate it through incantation, "Poughkeepsie."

"That's the place," Joe confirmed.

"So, mind if I take a look inside?" By now Eliot had fully regretted accepting Joe's invitation to see the house, and was hoping that the sooner he entered the sooner he could exit. Joe, on the other hand, took Eliot's initiative as genuine interest.

"Sure, sure, sure! Please!" He turned to lead Eliot into the house.

Eliot, however, was not interested in buying a house. Or, more precisely, he hadn't yet considered that he might be interested. This house, the house of Eliot's great-grandparents, was once part of the vibrant Slovenian-Catholic neighborhood of St. Vitus's Parish—a refuge for people displaced by the ravages of The Great War. Now abandoned to the twenty-first-century No Man's Land between downtown and East Cleveland, it was not quite as heavily defended by bolt-action rifles, mustard gas, and stick grenades as the few meters between enemy trenches dug into Flanders Field, but it was as cankered with fire and debris and wasted lives.

From the time his great-grandparents bought the house in 1922 until they moved out in 1947 (the year following the Cleveland Indians' move from Dunn Field to Municipal Stadium on the shores of Lake Erie) that small section of Northeast Ohio was idyllic. Property values were reasonably high then, and when they sold their home to an airplane pilot who was hired as the inaugural director of the newly opened Burke Lakefront Airport, the first municipally owned-and-operated airfield in the United States, they were able to purchase a single-story suburban bungalow with their own view of the lake. The sale even allowed them to properly celebrate the marriage of their youngest, Eliot's grandmother, to a man with no relation but the same last name. Over three hundred people attended the reception.

The house was damnably hot. Eliot stepped out of his unlaced boots and sunk into the plush carpet. Still, he towered over Joe's hunched frame. He unclasped the six buttons that ran down the front of his flannel shirt and peeled it off one arm at a time, revealing a yellow Squirts T-shirt, which he bought from the sale rack at Music Saves Record Shop on Waterloo Road after seeing a CLE-Punk cover band at the Beachland Tavern.

The fog of history clouded Eliot's glasses as if the morning's mist had been invited to follow the men indoors. He pulled the glasses from his ears, wrapped the hem of his T-Shirt around each lens, and polished them between thumb and forefinger before setting them back upon his nose. The air was rich with the unexpected smell of poppy-seed cake and powdered sugar. He became homesick for a home that was not his, but that now made a viable claim on the collective biography of his maternal lineage. Joe had made his way into the center of the room and was pointing to a mahogany upright piano.

"Bill Ivers built that piano in Boston three years before partnering with Handel Pond in 1880. It's worth more than the house! And actually, there was a Baldwin Acrosonic in that exact spot when I moved in. It must have been too much trouble to move, and not worth very much. This one, though, I inherited from an uncle, my father's twin brother, in 1960. That piano changed my daughter's life.

Eliot caught about every third or fourth word Joe had said. He deduced that they were not alone in the house, and that the yet to be identified party was rolling a beer keg down a flight of unseen stairs.

When the rolling keg came to a temporary rest Joe explained, "Sorry about that; it's the radiator. Sounds like someone whacking the pipes with a wrench." Joe was right. The bouncing keg was actually a more precise *whack* of steel against steel.

"They don't do that if you open the valves all the way," Eliot said.

"It gets too hot in here if I open the valves all the way. Plus—"

"It's a horror show," Eliot said.

"It's thermal expansion," said Joe. "The valves have nothing to do with it." He smiled and proceeded toward the kitchen. "Like I was saying, my daughter learned to play on that piano when she was eight years old. I think initially she just liked sitting at it. She always preferred pretty things. Jane, that's her name, she loved George Gershwin. "Rhapsody in Blue" over and over until she finally discovered the women: Clara Schumann and Fanny Mendelssohn, mostly. Eventually she began writing her own nocturnes. Women make better art than men, don't you think?"

Eliot shrugged. "Probably." Then unthinkingly added, "My mother was an artist."

Joe pulled out a chair for Eliot and moved toward the sink. "Tea?" he asked, not having heard Eliot's attempt to resurrect the memory of his mother above the running water.

"No, thank you," said Eliot, "I'm more of a coffee guy."

Joe had already begun filling a stainless steel kettle with tap water. The kettle was covered in yellow-brown flecks of scorched olive oil that had been baked into the metal over decades of use. Having screwed shut the knob to stop the faucet, Joe set the kettle on the gas range and opened the pilot.

"My Jane studied music composition and mathematics at The Oberlin Conservatory and The University of Chicago," He continued. Eliot figured this was impressive, and wondered if the old house still contained any of the magic that had vanished Joseph Kowalski's daughter from this depressed city. "Now she teaches Harmony at Vassar College."

"Where?" Eliot asked.

"New York," Joe said.

"Poughkeepsie," Eliot concluded, still unsure where that might be, but figuring, incorrectly, that it is a quaint up-state college town.

"That's right," Joe said. The kettle began its soft whistle, which quickly crescendoed into an alarming squeal. He pulled the kettle from the burner and turned off the gas then poured the boiling water into two mugs. The decaffeinated Earl Grey tea bags he had placed in each floated to the top before sinking among the tendrils of their own brown murk. Grabbing hold of the string and paper label, he jounced the bags through the thin, swirling film of Bergamot oil before landing one mug in front of Eliot and relaxing into a vacant chair across the table with his own in hand. Joe amazingly shrugged his already hunched shoulders even further and propped his elbows atop the kitchen table to the accompaniment of a series of creaks and pops. Eliot accepted the unwanted beverage with a nod and leaned back in the wooden chair, daring it to splinter.

Eliot absently brought the scalding tea to his lips. Before the liquid could burn his tongue, he paused, eyes peering over the crest of the mug at a series of names carved into the doorframe that led into a tiny washroom that would not have permitted even the smallest child very much room to maneuver. He tried not to imagine the contortions Joe suffered in that space.

Following Eliot's gaze to the carved molding, Joe's eyes beamed with the anticipated thrill of telling another story. Eliot noted the tired droop of the man's face: his eyes, though, were brilliant blue pools flanked by the cracked hardpan of a desert drought. Those eyes had won and lost Joseph Kowalski Senior each of his three wives.

From his position perched atop a rickety chair about ten feet from the bathroom, Eliot could read only the elegant letters obviously carved by an amateur woodworker that spelled out "LaRose." Joe, on the other hand, couldn't read anything at that distance, but knew by heart every name on that list. In his younger days Joe had been a history teacher, and in many ways he never really retired, as Eliot was in the process of discovering. Joe graduated from Kent State University in 1942 with a Bachelor's degree in History. To further defer conscription, he immediately enrolled as a graduate student in his department's terminal Masters Program along with seventeen other able-bodied young men. As a turn-of-the-century Americanist Joe was not the least bit interested in traveling to Europe, or, worse yet, the South Pacific. He wrote his Master's Thesis on early U.S. Government patents, including the application for the first hand-crank pasta machine, which was invented in Cleveland's Little Italy by Angelo Vitantonio in 1906. His thesis advisor, who also served on the Cleveland Board of Education, offered Joe a position as a full-time teacher for the Western Reserve Historical Society over the celebratory drinks that followed his defense. Joe began working as a liaison to the Cleveland Public Schools in the summer of 1947, and had been telling stories ever since.

"I bought this house in 1948. The Indians won the World Series that year, you'll recall," Joe said, simultaneously lifting his eyes and a finger toward Eliot's cap, which had been passed down to him by his great-grandfather, the previous owner of the house. It was in near tatters now, but it was authentic, and Eliot liked that most about it. "I never had a sit down like this with the previous owner," Joe continued, "He had been in the house less than a year when he crashed his plane somewhere along the Pulitzer Trophy Race Course. LaRose, was his name. Of course it was Odom's crash in '49 that finally put an end to the races in Cleveland."

"The what?" Eliot asked.

"The National Air Races. It was a cross-country affair that finished at the airport. Now it's out in the desert. Reno. But there was a shorter circuit race from Cleveland to Indianapolis and back. That was the Pulitzer."

"Never heard of it," Eliot said.

"Anyhow, the bank was foreclosing, and that list of names scratched into the door frame was five persons shorter. I was able to buy this place on the cheap. Unfortunately, I'm selling it for even cheaper."

Eliot leveled his chair, rose, and strode across the kitchen. Ned, Mary, Ruth, Yuri, Muriel, Florence, Jacob, Charlie, Madeline, 1st Lt. LaRose, Joseph, Mary, Emily, Abigail, Junior, Jane. He traced with his index finger the name Yuri. Then Muriel. Florence. Jacob. Charlie. Madeline.

"That Yuri, I think, is a Slavic name. It means George," Joe offered.

Eliot turned from the frame, the tip of his index finger still hanging in the crook of the final "e" that completed his grandmother's name: *Madeline.* She was born by the steady hand of a midwife in the simple, well-lighted kitchen he now stood. Her daughter and his mother would die in a hospital bed in the birthing ward of St. Vincent Charity Hospital forty-four years later.

"Do you know anything about him? Yuri?" Eliot asked.

"I did a bit of research a while back and found out that the name originated with Yuriy Dolgorukiy, the Grand Prince of Kiev. He founded Moscow. His great-grandfather...um, ah...oh, yes, Yaroslav the Wise, was the first Russian ruler who took Saint George as his patron." Joe finished.

"I meant the man who carved this." Eliot said.

An Historiography of Love in Three Parts: I
July 8, 1895

ELIOT'S GREAT-GRANDFATHER, Yuri Zupančič, was born after only a single hour of effortless labor in a two-room stone house numbered 51. He entered the world in his parents' second floor bedroom, which overlooked a mostly dirt yard only twice the size of their bed. The house stood on a modest farm at the edge of the village Velika Loka, in Austria-Hungary—then Yugoslavia, now Slovenia. Patrons at the Post Office a quarter mile down the road heard him test out his new lungs. His mother pulled him close to her bare breast and he quieted. His father held his wife's hand, and they smiled at one another, happy to have created something where once there was nothing.

Yuri grew up on the farm, which his father sold to his good friend, Janez, less than one year after the evening of Yuri's birth. Yuri's father was not as talented an agriculturalist as Janez, and so he improved his farm the only way he knew how: he transferred the deed for 125 krones and the promise that Janez would not only provide his family with room and board, but would also eat with them at the same table. Uncle Janez, as he became known to Yuri, had no family of his own and was more than happy to spend all of his time tending the land and feeding his friends. They ate sweet corn, zucca squash, radishes, rutabaga, parsnips, purple carrots, huckleberry potatoes, rhubarb, Armenian cucumbers, shallots, mustard greens, red cabbage, cauliflower, runner beans, and,

Yuri's favorite, drunken woman frizzy headed butter lettuce. They never farmed an animal, Yuri learned, because it was both disturbingly unethical and blighted the land.

Yuri had spent his entire childhood toddling around the farm, tending his own small row of beans that grew upon a line his mother helped him string above the earth on wooden stakes next to the house. When Yuri reached the age of accountability, he was sent to school where he would study to become a Catholic priest. The school was a little more than a one-hour hike from the farm in Velika Loka. The trail was not simple for a boy just past his seventh birthday. Yuri, however, walked the steep, rough roads with religious devotion from 1902 to 1909: half of his life. During that time, he only missed three days of class. Yuri was confirmed into the Catholic Church in 1904 at the Church of Saint James in Višnja Gora; he dutifully made his First Confession the following year. He received his First Holy Communion on August 5, 1906. Eliot's great-grandfather did not want to become a priest.

Yuri completed primary school and returned to work on the small farm his father had sold thirteen years earlier. He was content on this piece of land. But talk about the Emperor Franz Josef's impending death and the imminent war that would surely follow troubled the town. As the world approached war, Yuri approached the age of conscription. It was 1912, he was seventeen, and therefore required to serve in the Austro-Hungarian Army. But Yuri was a farmer, not a soldier. He planted seeds, and through the alchemy of sunlight and rain, cultivated crops to feed his small village. Life was a beautiful mystery to Yuri. He neither wanted to die, nor to kill. And so, instead of enlisting, he lied.

With permission from his parents, Yuri applied for a passport so that he could escape to the United States. The procedure included a false promise to the Austro-Hungarian government that he would return from America after three years to serve in the Army. Yuri's father wrote to his brother-in-law, Jacob, who had moved to Eveleth, Minnesota three years earlier to ask for funds to send Yuri to stay with his family. "If Yuri can get a passport to leave Austria legally, then I will finance the trip," Jacob's letter said. And so, with financial assistance from uncle, Yuri sailed for America on the Franz Josef I from the port of Trieste on June 6, 1912. Those were to be three of the most brutal and marvelous years of his life.

The ship carrying Eliot's great-grandfather to the United States and, ultimately, to the tall house in Cleveland, Ohio, made two stops along its trans-Atlantic voyage. It docked briefly at Patras, Greece, to pick up cargo and hapless asylum-seekers, beardless young men like Yuri silently escaping certain death in the brewing European war. Then the ship churned further from happiness through the furious Adriatic Sea toward Algiers, where coal was loaded like black mountains beneath the deck. The crew shoveled those mountains of anthracite rock without pause the remaining 192 hours of the trans-Atlantic voyage. They heaved and pitched and sweated and groaned, feeding the ship's boilers, propelling the emigrant cargo—dying of cholera, typhus, and dysentery, but not of nationalism—across the stormy Mediterranean Sea and hushed Atlantic Ocean.

On July 19th, 1912, the steam ship Franz Josef I arrived in New York Harbor under the watchful gaze of Lady Liberty—steadfast even against the glare of early morning sunshine reflecting off the placid water. The ship's passengers sat in waiting for nine hours. Yuri leaned against the railing, watching fellow immigrants from other vessels file down their gangways like cattle into the corrals at Ellis Island. He disembarked at 5:19 P.M., and two hours later he had passed a thorough physical examination. When he was asked to provide proof that he carried with him at least twenty-five U.S. dollars Yuri produced from the inside pocket of his overcoat a stout, sand-colored envelope. On the once smooth front face his father had written "125 Krones / 1896." Before he departed from Velika Loka, Yuri had written beneath his father's note on the now worn envelope, "125 Krones = $25.20 / 1912."

A brusque inspection official dispassionately stamped the processing paperwork that welcomed Yuri to America, and with no fanfare asked, "Destination?"

"Eveleth, Minnesota," Yuri answered. "To visit my Uncle Jacob."

"New York–Albany Line," The official said, and turned his attention to the woman standing in line behind Yuri.

Yuri stepped past a man who didn't look very different from himself, and briefly rested his hand on the man's shoulder in recognition of their mutual accomplishment. The man stood alone behind a large sign that read, "Ferry to the Central Railroad of New Jersey." Yuri continued left toward a longer line that wound around the Great Hall terminating before the placard reading "Ferry to Manhattan—Grand Central Station." An American flag adorned with forty-eight stars had been placed between those two ferry terminals fifteen days earlier on the Fourth of July, 1912.

The Ellis Island Ferry docked at Battery Park, exactly four miles from Grand Central Station. Yuri set one foot in front of the other up Broadway, intoxicated with wanderlust. A sign at the edge of the park declared in bold white letters on a luminous red background: "New York, The Wonder City!" The place seethed like no other. He felt as if still aboard the ferry, propelled by some vehicle larger than himself through the streets of Lower Manhattan. Even before he made it as far as the New York Stock Exchange, Yuri spied The Woolworth Building—complete except for a single turret on the northwest corner—lording over Park Row. The size of it blew back the curtains of his mind. He became unmoored, staring up into the great expanse of the New York skyline. The crowds around him were similarly disorientating: the explosion of street vendors, the jostling advance-and-retreat of pedestrians more familiar with the strange network of thoroughfares and alleyways. The dense army of traffic obscured the ground before him. He felt the dread of an infantry charge shake his knees.

The merciful blast of a kazoo offered Yuri his bearings. The crowd parted a few sidewalk slabs ahead of him to reveal a man singing in Yuri's native tongue! The bearded man marched in a small circle to delineate the boundary of his performance. Each step worked the arm of a drum by pulling taut a piece of clothesline that ran from his ankle to the drum squarely secured upon his back. A tambourine rattled atop his opposite foot. He strummed a guitar and squawked a horn, and when he wasn't singing, or blasting the kazoo, he hummed into a harmonica that rested upon a holder in front of his lips. For all the splendor of New York City this anonymous man and his band of instruments was the kindest gift that Eliot's great-grandfather could have received that afternoon.

Yuri hummed the man's song the rest of the way to Grand Central Station, and when he arrived, confirmed aloud to himself that everything about the aptly named building was indeed grand—including the trains and the people they carried. He brushed his shaggy black hair from his eyes and stood awash in a cluster of sunlight beaming through the high windows in the main hall, an awe-filled spectator of the choreographed arrival and departure of nearly five million bleary souls. When his train was announced on the magnificent departures marquee, Yuri realized that he was not a mere spectator, but a player in this scene. The epiphany filled him with a sense of urgent responsibility. He shoved off the tiled wall and joined the coarse throngs darting toward their trains.

Yuri rode the New York Central Railway through Albany to the Lake Shore & Michigan Southern lines before tramping a freight car on the Milwaukee Railroad—including the recently completed St. Paul Extension. He stayed in Eveleth for only two days, less time than it took him to walk from St. Paul to the mining town. Prior to his arrival, Yuri's Uncle Jacob had attempted and failed to get him employment in the underground iron ore mines where he worked as a pit-level motorman. Motormen were required to be at least twenty-one years old. Yuri had just turned seventeen. Jacob's supervisor, Herb Vickers, had said would be more successful at the Hibbing open pit mines where the age requirement was only eighteen. Even though the law was not strictly enforced, standard practice being to simply ask men to state their age at the time of being hired, Jacob thought Yuri had a better chance of passing inspection in Hibbing.

So, Yuri traveled to Hibbing, where Herb put in a good word for him with the Captain of the Number 4 Service Mine. The Captain was rightfully suspicious of Herb's note.

"You don't look eighteen," He said, lightly smacking Yuri's smooth cheek with an open hand.

"I'm a close shaver," Yuri insisted.

The captain laughed and assigned him as a brakeman on the surface. A motorman, like his Uncle Jacob, would haul iron ore from a network of underground chutes to the mineshaft where the ore was then hoisted to the surface by the brakeman. Yuri earned $2.10 per eight-hour day, plus burial expenses in case of death. He was never asked to kill another man or to sleep in a flooded trench next to rotting corpses and rabid rats. He was so happy.

Then, one evening in late-October, 1912, Eliot's great-grandparents fell in love. Yuri was enjoying an after-work beer at his boarding house when he heard her voice. It was like the warm, earthy tones of a bassoon. He quickly scanned the crowd, and his eyes caught her clapping hands and smiling face that would forever quicken his heart. Her name was as beautiful as her happiness: Muriel.

The war began in Europe, and American iron ore mines that had seemed until then a world away from the Front lost all standing orders. Yuri's company was forced to lay off all single men in order to give preference to workers with families. Yuri was forced to leave Hibbing and Muriel.

"Wait for me," he asked.

"I will," she promised.

Yuri spent a quarter of his savings on transportation to International Falls, Minnesota, a lumber camp stationed at the Canadian border 104 miles from his fiancée. With some luck, he was able to get work at a small cedar camp that specialized in cutting, skidding, and processing oak railroad ties. In the summer months the forest was swampy and there were so many mosquitoes that the men had to cover their faces with two layers of cloth to keep from breathing in the insects. Still, their teeth were black with bugs. They worked with their eyes nearly closed against the thick smog of a billion pests. One evening Yuri suggested they burn green leaves to drive the hoards away. It was no remedy, and the smoke became so thick they nearly suffocated in it. *So this is what it is like to be gassed*, Yuri thought. Again, he was wrong.

The winter months were no better. The temperature dropped to thirty degrees below zero. Surprisingly, no one starved, but everyone was hungry. At night they happily recalled the summer months when they would dig up potatoes and cabbage in the early morning without the farmers' permission. To boil the little food they had the crew kept a fire continuously burning near the center of camp. One man was in charge of brewing coffee and boiling clothes all day long. Yuri would thaw his frozen fingers on a blistering cloth that hung before the fire, but it was the thought of Muriel that kept him warm.

Despite the difficult condition the work was consistent and Yuri enjoyed his job. On the last day of February, however, Yuri and a Polish boy named Michael were loading timbers onto a box car when one of them rolled onto Yuri's hand and smashed his finger. Michael quickly dislodged the flattened digit and escorted Yuri to the emergency tent where the doctor wanted to cut off the portion that was smashed. Yuri thought of Muriel's hand interlaced with his and refused. After a few days, infection set in and he was unable to work for three weeks. The camp boss charged him such an ungodly rate for room and board in the infirmary that Yuri was able to save only $20.00 from nearly four months of work. He angrily quit, and when Michael found out what had happened, he also left the timber trade.

Michael had heard that farms in North Dakota were already beginning to hire summer help, so he and Yuri decided to head west. It was still too early in the season to harvest grain, but Michael thought they might get a job making hay. With only a small sum between them, the two men walked thirty miles on railroad tracks, stepping from one tie to the next, in hopes of catching a free ride on a freight train. They encountered a number of temporary farmers and hobos who were also looking for free transport. The two men traveled a sideline of the Northern Pacific Line that didn't see much traffic in the early spring, but a section gang told them that a westbound train would likely pass in a day or two. Later that afternoon a town appeared in the distance. Yuri said that it resembled pier posts rising up out of the ocean at Ellis Island. Michael recalled the red poppy fields of Poland, which, unbeknownst to him, had recently been trampled, burned, and trenched.

The men arrived in the town under nightfall to find that two trains were scheduled to leave the yard just after midnight: one heading north to Canada and one west toward North Dakota. To successfully tramp the train, they had to go out some distance from the yard and jump aboard the train while it was already in in motion. As they daringly vaulted aboard what they hoped was the westbound train to North Dakota, a dense cloud thick as motor oil daubed the town, suffocating any moonlight that tried to pervade its murk. In the pitch black neither man could read the train's identifying lettering. The boxcar was empty and the men were exhausted. They slept.

The next morning Eliot's great-grandfather woke up to find the train had stopped. Looking out the open door, he saw Canadian Railroad policemen and a sign that read "Emerson, Canada." His toes curled and his scrotum tightened. His tensed muscles held him prisoner. The police spotted him immediately. Unable to flee, he was taken inside the station for questioning. Yuri was rightfully frightened. His identifying paperwork and accent betrayed him as Austrian, and Canada was at war with Austria and Germany. He feared detention and worse, deportation. He thought of all the luck that had delivered him to this moment, and the vital star removed from the fragile constellation of his life that might be lost forever. The policeman informed Yuri that he was now a prisoner of war under the suspicion of espionage, and that he would be detained at a Canadian internment camp.

"Muriel," Yuri wept.

Through his tears Yuri insisted that both he and Michael, whom he had not seen since their acrobatics the previous evening, were on their way to harvest grain in North Dakota and that he was not a spy. He told them that he had already taken out first citizenship papers in the United States with the intention of becoming an American citizen in 1917, once he had been in residence a full five years. The policemen asked to see the papers.

"I've left them with my fiancée in Hibbing," he told them.

They exchanged a doubtful grimace. "Where did you get your initial citizenship papers?" they asked.

"At the County Office of St. Louis in Minnesota," Yuri said.

The Canadian Railroad Police dispatched a telegram to the St. Louis Courthouse and received verification in return, which they took as acceptable corroboration of Yuri's story. Satisfied that he had entered Canada by error and that he was not dangerous, the policemen escorted Yuri over the border to the American side of the railroad yard and loaded him on the next freight train south. He never learned what happened to Michael.

As soon as he arrived in Minnesota, Yuri reunited with Muriel and the two of them moved to Eveleth, where a job had opened for him at the Kohler Company foundry alongside his soon-to-be father-in-law. Yuri would manufacture bathroom fixtures for the next five years. Steel dust from filing, grinding, and sand blasting would hang constant in the air, working its way into his lungs and underpants.

The couple was married immediately upon their arrival in Eveleth on November 20, 1916. Since Muriel's father was against the marriage, they did not have a wedding reception; instead they enjoyed a simple dinner with a few close friends. It was customary at that time to get married on a Monday, so even though Yuri didn't ask his future father-in-law's permission, he did have to ask his foreman for the day off.

"If you don't show up on Tuesday, consider yourself fired," he obliged.

News of Yuri's marriage did not reach his parents in the Versailles State until after the *Armistice of Compiègne* took effect ceremoniously at 11:00 A.M. on November 11, 1918. The news brought as much joy to the small farm in Velika Loka as the end of the War. Yuri's parents were also anxious to meet his new wife, but Yuri refused to leave the country until his family became full United States citizens.

On January 15, 1920 Yuri received his United States citizen's documents along with papers for Muriel and their first daughter, Florence. That was the earliest date that citizens' papers were issued to Austrians following The Great War. A year later he passed his examination for citizenship and applied for an American passport. On May 21, 1921, Yuri, Muriel, and their new baby left Minnesota on a train headed for New York City, where they would then travel to Yugoslavia aboard the same ship that brought Yuri to the United States in 1912: The Franz Josef I. They planned to stop in Cleveland, Ohio, for one week to visit Muriel's Aunt Bernadette.

Inauguration
October 4, 2013

CORNELL FISHED a new, plastic disposable lighter from atop the few crumpled dollar bills that formed a plush nest at the bottom of his pant pocket. His ashy brown knuckle bent, stretching taut the unique fissures that creased his arthritic knob. The underside of his thumb dimpled and snapped across the serrated steel wire of the lighter's sparkwheel, generating sparks like smoldering confetti. Cornell's thumb came to a rest on the red fork. Butane vapors ascended to meet the falling sparks. A flame combusts and takes its shape: a sea anemone swaying in the undercurrent.

Cornell introduced the dancing flame to the joint tucked between cockled lips. The thin, white rice paper began to fester as he sucked the flame's heat through the now unveiled green and purple Hindu Kush. The fire quickly scorched the dried cellulose leaves, releasing an unadulterated turbid white smoke that smelled of sour mandarin and Ichang papeda. The smoldering leaves glowed luminous like the hollowed-out eye sockets of a jack-o-lantern. A rogue cinder absconded like a comet, cooled in mid-flight, and vanished. Another escaped, then disappeared. Cornell drew the smoke through the joint and into his mouth. It was luscious. He cradled the cream with his tongue, arousing his taste buds with the tart flavor of over-ripe yuzu.

He swallowed the smoke into his lungs. Cornell held his breath to detain the smoke while the drug was collected and redistributed into the shipping lanes of his bloodstream, finally delivering a dose of euphoria to his brain. His heart quickened, beating in double time, keeping pace with Ringo's tumbadora on "A Day in the Life," which his friend, Frank Hopkins, had queued up on the reel-to-reel machine. It had been there since Frank purchased it from an antique shop in Willoughby in 1999. Cornell leaned back into his chair and coughed forth a swell of smoke that looked to Frank like the billowing eruption of Mount St. Helens.

The loud cough met Eliot's ears as he walked past Cornell's 1973 sage-green Norton Commando 750 that leaned habitually against the pox-marked brick wall near the rear-entry door of Big Sleep Books. Eliot stalled for a moment to remember the loving hum of the bike's twin engine between his legs as he sped across mile after mile of quiet Ohio farmland. The massive two point five inch, sixteen-gauge top rail frame designed by former Rolls Royce engineers, housed twin Amal concentric carburetors and a four-speed gearbox that, under Eliot's direction, had recently barnstormed Midwestern back roads from University Heights to Willa Cather's childhood home in Red Cloud, Nebraska, at a steady 95 miles per hour.

Eliot leaned his thick shoulder into the heavy oak door that opened into the apartment he shared with his father at the back of the shop. He immediately detected the mild avant-garde effluvium of citrused marijuana smoke. The scent intensified as he walked through the studio apartment toward an unbolted door leading into the bookstore. He swung it wide, allowing smoke and sound to diffuse into the hall. "A Day in the Life" had reached the alarming conclusion of its orchestral bridge, twenty-three bars that always possessed Eliot with a sense of impermanence. The doorway deposited him into a cramped space behind the counter with Cornell and his father.

"Not expecting any customers today?" Eliot smiled at two stoned men.

"Eliot Ness, the untouchable!" Cornell offered his usual greeting. He shifted his left buttocks as if to release a primed fart, but instead attempted to pass Eliot the joint now pinched between his fingers. Eliot waved him off.

"Cops use the front door, CT," Eliot said, disowning the moniker. The two had known each other since Eliot was eight years old when Cornell became his father's best friend and employee.

Frank—who had named his son after his hero, the famous Chicago-based Prohibition Agent and, later, Cleveland's Safety Director—seemed to have fallen asleep in his wheelchair with all the grace of a waffle iron.

"Hey, Pop," Eliot tested.

Frank's heavy eyelids remained sagged into his cheeks, but he acknowledged his son's salutation with a halcyon smile and a thumb jabbed toward the ceiling. The song mellowed into its third act, inquiring about the number of holes it might take to fill the Albert Hall before the reel-to-reel machine clicked into reverse, winding the tape back onto the left wheel.

Eliot sat himself atop the empty barstool next to Cornell and a large stack of recently acquired used books that needed to be shelved in the basement. From his perch, Eliot took stock of the shelves labeled with hand-made signs, oversized index cards marked with black sharpie print from 'Ancient Thrillers' to 'Vatican Secrets.' To his surprise a pair of teenaged girls sat cross-legged on the floor in front of the 'Whodunits,' a new trade-paperback copy of Agatha Christie's *Murder on the Orient Express* open between them. Eliot shot Cornell a look as if a fart cloud had actually disturbed his olfactory. Cornell puckered his right eye, which distorted the entire side of his face as if to say, "Nah, man, don't even worry about them." Eliot silently pressed his friend.

"Better to get high in here with Agatha than smoking themselves stupid in the mall parking lot or wherever," Cornell whispered. The reel-to-reel had finished rewinding and began to play the opening riffs of *Sgt. Pepper's Lonely Hearts Club Band.*

Eliot opened his mouth to respond, but conceded that Cornell's logic was fairly sound. Two bookstores set the boundaries of Coventry Village: Big Sleep at the south end, and Revolution on the north side. In between, Cleveland's hipper sub-cultures thrived: free thinkers, free spirits, free loaders. It was Cleveland's less significant Haight-Ashbury. A place so rusted and neglected—except for the few dilatants living above the head shops and record stores lining both sides of the street, and the proprietors of those establishments who performed a daily homage to San Francisco cool—that Cornell and Frank could openly smoke in the chilled out context of their dusty, used bookstore without reservation.

Eliot scanned the upstairs loft that wrapped around the side and back walls of the store and that was glutted with uncategorized, two-dollar copies of one-time bestsellers procured from any number of Cuyahoga County Public Library used-book sales. He leaned into the backrest and kicked his feet up atop the counter. Eliot removed his cap and tossed it on the counter, letting his hair fall messily around his ears, then returned his attention to Cornell who had open before him a graphic novel that would soon be shelved in the basement with the other Sherlock Holmes paraphernalia. "What's that?" he asked.

"*Victorian Undead,*" Cornell said without looking up. "Professor Moriarty's a zombie."

Cornell had introduced Eliot to the zombie genre via George Romero's *Night of the Living Dead* when he was thirteen years old. Eliot was fascinated. Not by Romero's flesh eaters, but by the inability of anyone—presumably capable scientists and the United States Military alike—to solve the mystery of how the dead had come back to life. His fascination grew into something of a Holmsian obsession. "Any answers?" Eliot asked.

"An alien disease carried to earth by a comet," Cornell said, well knowing to what Eliot referred.

Eliot, as per usual, refused the alien postulate. "The Samsa Dilemma endures," he said, shaking his head. Eliot had proposed his own theory of the zombie-narrative-as-detective-story after reading the famously disorientating opening of Franz Kafka's *The Metamorphosis* in which Gregor Samsa wakes up one morning to find himself transformed into a giant cockroach, and recognized its parallel to the way popular zombie fictions open with the convenient coming-to of a coma patient.

"True. True. But why can't the alien thing work?" Cornell asked, well-knowing Eliot's hang-up. The two girls had exited the store unnoticed and pleasantly high. They left the now-used paperback upon the floor.

"Aliens aren't real." Eliot slid off his stool to retrieve the book, which he worked into the interstice between *Murder on the Links* and *The Mysterious Mr. Quin.* "I guess I have to get on board with the fact that the threat of an exotic, solitary figure is less terrifying than the horror of an anonymous, shambling mass culture," Eliot said.

"I don't know about all that, man. Every book in this dust bin is predicated upon an exotic, solitary figure," Cornell said.

"*Touché, mon frère,*" Eliot said.

"Are you taking a piss?" Cornell asked.

"Not at all. Look, you asked about "The Samsa Dilemma." Zombie stories all begin the same way: waking up to a cataclysmic change without having any clue as to what's going on, thus aligning zombies with the modern detective story." Eliot said. "Except nobody's on the case to figure out exactly what happened to set the whole thing in motion."

"And that's a problem," Cornell stated more than asked.

"It is if your dad owns a bookstore that specializes in 'Cops, Spies, and Private Eyes,'" Eliot said. "We are in the business of selling books, right?"

Cornell dropped the seething roach into the deep bend of his calabash pipe ringed with a Meerschaum cup stained to the yellow blush of a Rainer Cherry, and dragged the final streams of marijuana through its oxidized stem. "*Touché*," he wheezed. He then lazily wedged a small stack of used books beneath his armpit and slugged his way past the staff recommendations to the top of the steps leading into the basement. His calabash still hanging from his jaw, Cornell said between clenched teeth, "The game is afoot," and descended the stairs.

Eliot shook his head lovingly at Cornell's ceremony of transforming the duty of shelving worn paperbacks into something that resembled a puzzle, and opened his copy of *The Amazing Adventures of Kavalier & Clay*. He indulged his habit of re-reading the final sentence of the chapter he had previously finished before moving on to new material:

> "The true magic of this broken world lay in the ability of the things it contained to vanish, to become so thoroughly lost, that they might never have existed in the first place."

He read the sentence a second time as if it were an incantation that might conjure all that had vanished from his life. He thought about the girl with ale-brown hair. He thought of his mother. He thought, too, of Yuri, whose signature was carved into the bathroom doorframe of Joseph Kowalski Senior's home on Cleveland's east side, but whose story lived inside him. Eliot turned the page by dragging the pressed pulp from right to left across the book's remaining chapters. The chafe produced its familiar *schuck* and *thwipp;* Frank slept loudly behind his son.

(Mis)Fortune
October 31, 1999

FRANK HOPKINS DREAMT of Halloween. The Cleveland sky
opened wide its insipid grayness and cast forth a legion of cold,
heavy raindrops. Winds off the lake plucked most of the
remaining leaves from their branches and deposited them on
rooftops and roadways all along the eerie coast. The waning
crescent of the late-autumn moon dipped below the western
horizon at 4:39 P.M., and the sun had followed at 6:21 P.M.
The night was black as an abandoned iron mine when Frank
Hopkins left Euclid Fire Station No. 1 at the end of his 24-
hour shift.

Frank's tired Honda Accord balked at his initial turn of the
key. The starter always acted up in wet conditions, but
eventually would yield to his persistence. On the fourth try, his
car rattled to life like a dog shaking water droplets from its
waterlogged pelt. He turned right out of the lot, away from his
own home that backed up to the Station's property, toward
Lakeshore Boulevard and his parents' house on E. 280th Street.
The curves and undulations of the boulevard were like a supine
body spread across the shoreline. Frank looked at the
dashboard clock: 7:03. He should be to his parents' home by
7:10 P.M. where he would retrieve his eight-year-old son for a
night of trick-or-treating.

The previous night, before Frank dropped Eliot off to
spend the evening with his grandparents, they had opened the
Plain Dealer to the weather section to check the Halloween

forecast. Eliot, already in his Christopher Robin costume consisting of a pale-yellow polo shirt and royal-blue cotton shorts, sat on his father's lap holding open a broad Cleveland Indians golf umbrella over their heads. Frank pointed to the illustrated rain clouds inked on the newspaper to which Eliot responded merrily and in character, "Tut-tut. It looks like rain!" Eliot did not realize he would have to wear his coat over his costume. He also didn't know what festivities were in store for him once they finished their march up and down the nearby streets: apple cider doughnuts, Euclid Beach popcorn balls, a pillowcase worth of candy spread out before them on Frank's old flannel Coleman sleeping bag, and Eliot's first viewing of *It's the Great Pumpkin, Charlie Brown*.

Frank pulled into the center lane, his left turn signal blinking its rapid swan song, when he noticed a stalled vehicle on the far-right shoulder just before Westbrook Drive. Someone had jacked up the back end of a late-model Chrysler sedan and was currently struggling with the lug nuts on the left-rear tire. Frank steered his Honda across two lanes, shiny with a mix of rain and oil, and parked behind the stranded motorist. He put on his flashers and exited into the rain.

Frank yelled, "Need some help?"

"Yeah, thanks," A man's voice responded. "I can't get any leverage."

"One second. I've got a torque wrench in the trunk," Frank said. He reached inside the car and pulled up on the truck release. He threw on his Euclid Fire Department rain slicker and grabbed the torque wrench along with an extender he had made out of a piece of steel fence rail.

"This ought to help," he said as he knelt down next to the man.

"Thanks."

"Not a problem," Frank assured him.

The man noticed the firefighter's patch on Frank's jacket and said, "Oh, sorry. I didn't even call anyone. It's not that big a deal."

"I'm off duty," Frank said. He had already finished removing the flat tire and was setting the doughnut in place. "And, you're right, it's not a big deal," Frank winked. He tightened down the only mildly stripped lug nuts and kicked the release on the jack.

"Hey, thanks again," the man said.

"No worries," Frank said. "Look, take it easy on that doughnut, though, especially in this weather. It doesn't really have any traction." The two men shook hands and the motorist drove off while Frank packed his gear back into the Honda's trunk next to an adult-sized Winnie-the-Pooh costume he rented to surprise Eliot.

He stole a look at his watch. 7:17 P.M. Eliot would no doubt be looking out the large front window of his grandparents' house, eager to see Frank pull into the driveway. Before he closed the trunk, Frank had to fish his fingers into the latching mechanism to manually flip the catch into the closed position. The return spring had fallen out sometime the previous summer and Frank couldn't justify the $23.95 it would cost for a new trunk latch assembly, a convenience that would really only save him about three seconds a couple of times each day.

It took about three seconds for Cornell Tillman to lose control of his penny-colored Mercury Zephyr, and hydroplane at 39 MPH into Frank Hopkins as he hunched over his trunk, manually flipping the broken catch into place. The impact cleaved Frank's left leg in two, and crushed his right into a sticky pulp of shattered bone; knotted tendons; and a stew of blood, skin, and urine. Frank, pinned between the crumpled front end of Cornell's Zephyr and the void of his Honda's trunk, passed out from the pain. His face sunk into the cozy fleece of Pooh's golden fur.

The paramedics arrived on the scene from Euclid Fire Station No. 1, and immediately set to work stabilizing Frank. He was airlifted to the Metro Hospital Trauma Center where his right leg was amputated above the knee, a job the Zephry's bumper had completed on his left leg an hour earlier. Cornell, on his way to an annual costume contest at Pat's in the Flats where he played bass in the house band, stepped from his freshly waxed Mercury dressed like a pimp and physically unscathed. He would never get behind the wheel of a car again.

He was taken to the Hospital as a precaution, tested for a concussion, and released. Cornell waited in the ICU for Frank to wake up from surgery, replaying the accident over and over again in his mind as a sort of mental flagellation. He was finally escorted into Frank's fluorescent room just after midnight. In the hallway, he passed an elderly couple, their faces pallid and uncertain, accompanied by a young boy wearing an outfit more suitable for a July day at Sim's Park than an October evening in the ER.

Cornell walked, trembling, into Frank's room. He was still dressed in a black velour jacket with leopard print lapels and matching pants. When he saw the half man smearing tears across his face with the undersides of his fingers, he, too, began to weep. Frank set a piece of folded orange construction paper on the table next to a small pile of Halloween candies, and offered Cornell his hand in hopes of consoling the man who had taken his legs. Cornell read the squiggly letters written in blue Crayola marker on the front of a homemade get-well card: "I love you, Dad!" His heart broke.

"Wrong place, wrong time, Prudent," Frank assured him.

Cornell looked at Frank, his face nebulous as though reflected in a pool of quivering water, and said, "*Je ne sais pas, monsieur. Je m'excuse.*"

Inauguration
October 4, 2013

FRANK AWOKE from the unprescribed spell of illicit pain relief. The setting sun became briefly visible as it dipped below the high snow clouds before performing its nightly vanishing act beneath the roofline of the parking garage across the street. Its final rays refracted though the front display window of Big Sleep Books, illuminating a swirling universe of dust. Frank rubbed at the phantom pains to ease his mind while Eliot, who had taken Cornell's place at the counter and was talking to a customer, finished the transaction.

"Hey, bud," Frank said when the customer exited the store.

Eliot spun on his stool to face his father, "Hey, pop." He watched as Frank groped at the air beneath his knees. "You doing okay today?" he asked."

"Yeah, I'm fine," Frank said. "Habit."

"Cornell picked up a couple of subs from Grums earlier. I put yours in the fridge. You want me to get it?"

"What time is it?" Frank asked.

"Couple minutes after seven," Eliot said.

"Yeah, thanks," Frank said, looking around for his friend. "Is Cornell still here?"

"No, the Papish Cats are playing at Night Town. First set is at 9:00. I guess he had an appointment at the Music Emporium, something about a new bridge for his upright. He left, maybe, fifteen minutes ago," Eliot said.

Frank unlocked the wheels of his chair and rolled from behind the counter to the front window where Dillinger, a nine-year-old black-and-white Great Dane, lay sprawled across the entire length of the store's futon basking in the lingering warmth of the declining sun. Frank named the enormous dog after the notorious Depression-era bank robber and prison-breaker, John Dillinger, declaring, "No cage will ever hold him!"

Eliot disappeared through the apartment door to fetch Frank's dinner.

Dillinger had been a gift from Cornell to commemorate the fifth anniversary of Big Sleep Books, which Frank started with the money from his disability pension as an homage to his dead wife. Cornell had worked with at the shop since the day it opened. The dog let out a series of high-pitched brays, his paws twitching over the edge of the mattress. His body pitched with the same lack of agility he would have put on display were he awake. Frank massaged Dillinger's velvet ear and kissed it. The dog calmed, then slowly opened the droop of his eyes. Still lying on his side, Dillinger stretched his limbs and produced an earnest yawn. The rank smell of his breath made Frank turn away.

"Ugh," he belched.

The dog responded by standing up, spinning in two quick circles to survey his landing space, and laid back down. He faced away from Frank, his limbs tightly tucked into his body and his head folded back almost to the pit of his crotch in order to conserve the heat he had collected from the now absent sun. One paw curled over the tip of his nose. Frank patted his rump.

Eliot returned with Frank's sandwich. He waved it in the air to let him know dinner was served, and plunked it down on the counter. "I've got the show tonight, so I'll probably take off in a few minutes myself," he said.

"Play some Geeshie Wiley, will ya?" Frank asked.

"Absolutely," Eliot said. "I'll start with 'Last Kind Words' so you don't have to tune in very late."

"That's the one," Frank said. He unfastened the masking tape and unrolled the sandwich paper across the counter, disarranging a stack of leftover 'Banned Books Week' bookmarks. "Listen, can you take Dillinger out before you leave?"

"Yep," Eliot said, and called to Dillinger, "Come on, pal. Let's go outside."

Dillinger's ears raised like the Flying Nun's habit, and his eyebrows shifted sweetly back-and-forth to locate the direction of Eliot's voice. Once he spotted the boy, he let out a fatigued groan and slowly stood up. His joints audibly creaked and popped. Dismounting his futon he stretched each back leg individually, allowing the second one to linger for a few moments before he dragged it down. The boy and dog exited Big Sleep Books through the door leading to Eliot and Frank's apartment. Dillinger led them the length of the hallway before arriving at the back door where Eliot slung a collar around the dog's neck. Dillinger bound into the chill of the back parking lot toward a small patch of grass next to the building. He hunched his back and settled in. The stench was visible, lending credibility to the term "Cleveland Steamer." Eliot laughed at the thought while his dog kicked at the frozen ground.

Eliot's fingertips began to ache from the cold. He blew hot breath into his clenched fists to temporarily relieve the small pain. Eliot's wristwatch sounded the hour. Danny Salazar (who at that moment stood upon the pitcher's mound before 43,345 zealous Cleveland Indians fans, prepared to heave his first career post-season pitch, a slider down and inside) also trumpeted a blast of warmth into his throwing hand. Eliot scooped up Dillinger's crud, pitched it into a nearby garbage can, and ushered him back inside.

"Hey, Dad. You want the game on before I leave?"

"Yeah, could you?" Frank unwound a length of blue paper and foil from a half empty pack of mints. He tossed one into his mouth and offered another to Eliot.

"Sure," he said, taking a mint. By the time Eliot pulled up News Radio WTAM 1100's live feed and clicked on the small laptop speakers DeJesus had already lined out to Center and Meyers had struck out swinging. First Baseman, James Loney had taken two strikes and was waiting on the third pitch.

"Sah-wiiiiing and a miss, strike three!" the Indians play-by-play announcer said. "That'll do it for the Rays in the top of the first. We're off to an auspicious start here in Cleveland!"

An Historiography of Love in Three Parts: II
May 28, 1921

YURI ZUPANČIČ'S YOUNG FAMILY arrived in Cleveland to find Bernadette and her husband Victor struggling mightily. A depression had taken hold throughout the Great Lakes States that would fester into something much greater by 1930. Neither Bernadette nor Victor were able to find work and their mortgage had backed up nearly seven months. Without hesitation Yuri sold his family's steam ship tickets to Velika Loka and handed the money over to his wife's aunt and uncle. He also contacted a man he had worked with in the Hibbing mines that now managed the warehouse at the United States Steel plant. Yuri was able to secure work in the stock room at the Cyclone Fence Company, where the starting pay was $0.40 per hour. He worked ten hours per day, six days per week. In September of that same year he was promoted to supervisor and he was able to hire Victor to fill his old position in the stock room. When he told Victor about the job, and shared the news that he and Muriel would stay in Cleveland through the winter to help with some home repairs and to save money for their return to Minnesota, his uncle was grateful. To thank his nephew, Victor took Yuri to see the Cleveland Indians play the New York Yankees at Dunn Field. On the evening of September 26, 1921, Eliot's great-grandfather attended his first baseball game.

It was the American League Pennant Game. Stan Coveleski stood on the pitcher's mound wearing a white uniform with navy blue letters that spelled out "Worlds Champions." His hat matched the one Victor had purchased for Yuri from the merchandise stand near the main gate at the corner of Lexington Avenue and East 66th Street: navy blue felt with an embossed white "C" above the bill. Yuri and Victor, along with 21,412 other proud Clevelanders, waved small replica pennants from last year's World Series victory, which the ushers handed out following the National Anthem. The air smelled of hope, equal parts stale beer and peanuts; the raked clay, the emerald grass, the billowing organ—doctrines of America. Yuri discovered the remarkable beauty of measuring, in balls, strikes, and outs, all the possibilities of life on the diamond.

As Coveleski prepared for the first pitch, massaging the rosin bag and digging a trench with his cleats in front of the rubber plate for better velocity, the public address announcer reminded the Cleveland hopeful that he had pitched three complete game winners in the Indians' best-of-nine World Series win over the Brooklyn Dodgers the previous year.

The winner of this game, which depended mostly on the junk of Coveleski's spitball, would win the American League Pennant and go on to play the New York Baseball Giants in the 1921 World Series. Coveleski was known around the league as "the gun at a knife fight": the youngest of only seventeen pitchers permitted to continue throwing baseballs doctored with anything from toothpaste to snot following the league's decision to ban the practice at the start of the 1921 season. Coveleski pulled his cap from his head, ran his fingers through blonde hair slick with vegetable oil, tugged the cap down to his eyebrows, and smeared the ball. His left knee, a piston, rose toward his chest, and his right foot sunk into the trench before the rubber plate exactly sixty feet and six inches from his catcher's glove. His hips cranked, his right knee locked, and he hurled the greased ball toward the Yankee already twisting in anticipation. The crowd roared!

Coveleski was pulled in the third inning, and the Indians' season ended with an 8-7 loss. The irony was not lost on Yuri, who had recently filed his citizenship papers: once again the Yankees has ousted the Indians from their rightful place in America. He wondered if history was doomed to repeat itself or if things eventually got better—or worse.

Their walk from Dunn Field to the house on Dibble Avenue took fewer than five minutes. Yuri, less disappointed by the loss than enchanted with the game, swung an imaginary bat and caught imaginary pop-flies and, with an emphatic pump of his fist called, "You're out!" He cupped both hands over his mouth and hissed from his throat to mimic the sound of 21,414 baseball fans cheering for the home team. Victor, less disappointed by the loss than pleased by how his nephew had so enthusiastically taken to the game, smiled a toothy grin revealing bits of candy-coated popcorn lodged between his teeth. He patted Yuri on the back before covering his own mouth with both hands to howl.

In the spring of 1922 Eliot's great-grandparents purchased the house at the corner of East 74th Street and Central Avenue where Eliot had sat with Joseph Kowalski Senior. For twenty-five years they lived a one-and-a-half-mile walk to Dunn Field. In the side yard, Yuri planted eight rows of grapes between two small crabapple trees. The following October he would harvest his first clusters and begin making his own wine in the cellar. Next to his fermenting barrels, Muriel jarred homemade jams.

Inauguration
October 4, 2013

"YOU'RE LISTENING TO 88.7 FM, WJCU, broadcasting live from the campus of John Carroll University in University Heights, Ohio. Request lines are open, so give me a call." Eliot kept the studio dark, choosing to run his show by the glow of computer monitors and the two-dozen red and yellow buttons that operated the digital mixing board. It felt correct and necessary to spin blues records about broken hearts and the broken people they belong to in the dark, letting the warm, low-end crackle of vintage vinyl light the space. The on-air booth also drew light through a window that shone into a seldom-used hallway running from the weight room to the bank of university mailboxes. Sometimes at this hour, students might traverse the hall from their dormitories across South Belvoir to The Underground for a late-night slice. A few years back the station had used a ration of its annual Radiothon Pledge Drive donations to install a speaker in the hallway just outside the studio window so that passers-by could hear the broadcast for the few seconds it took to walk the hall. It was a marketing ploy that had done little more than incite drunken frat boys to bang on the window like children demanding that a caged zoo animal acknowledge their existence. Eliot hated the window and the speaker. He was certain that neither would ever prove useful.

Eliot slid the volume dials a fraction closer to zero. The Hot Sardines' rendition of "Bei Mir Bist du Schoen" played delicately beneath his top-of-the-hour announcements: "It's 28 degrees at

2:04 A.M. according to the temperature measurements coming in from Hopkins International Airport, though Cleveland feels just a bit cooler than that after the Indian's season-ending 4-0 loss to the Tampa Bay Devil Rays." The usual background tracks were provided by Herb Alpert and the Tijuana Brass, but Cornell had recently given Eliot a bootleg copy of *The Hot Sardines Live at Joe's Pub*, which he had picked up while on a week-long tour of East Village jazz clubs with the Papish Cats.

"Before the news break we heard a pair from Robert Johnson: 'Me and the Devil Blues' and 'Hellhound on My Trail.' Both tracks were laid down during Johnson's final recording session, which took place over two days in 1937. The interesting thing about Robert Johnson's brand of Delta Blues, and really turn-of-the-century blues more generally, was his fascination with and appropriation of the Faust myth. *Faust* has its roots in a thirteenth-century play about a cleric who is said to have sold his soul in exchange for an ecclesiastical position." The phone lines began blinking red with lonely, late-night listeners wanting to philosophize with Eliot about the American racialization of Satan, or the various locations of the mythical Mississippi crossroads—Hazelhurst, Beauregard, Rosedale, Beulah. Eliot ignored the feeble persistence of the flickering lights until they had silently burnt out, one-by-one.

"Washington Irving's 'The Devil and Tom Walker' in the nineteenth century, and Stephen Vincent Benét's 'The Devil and Daniel Webster,' written the same year Johnson recorded his diabolical tracks, helped relocate the European Dr. Faustus to rural New England." As he spoke, Eliot readied the next record.

He let *Alice* fall from its protective sleeve into his hand, and gracefully flipped it so that Side A was positioned to accept the needle. He dropped the needle arm near the patent leather edge of the disc. It relaxed into one of the initial grooves of pressed vinyl, and Eliot heard Tom Waits sing through his headphones, "You waved your crooked wand..."

He stopped the record's rotation and manually spun it in the opposite direction to queue up the song's opening growl, which delivered Eliot a glut of nostalgia: A dimly lit Aurora farmhouse; the mesmerizing musk of dirt and pine emanating from the wood-burning stove; a French 75, his first bohemian cocktail; an albino kitten; the enchanting paean about a girl named Alice.

"Now here's the title track from Tom Waits's 2002 release, *Alice*, which he wrote for Robert Wilson's absurdist staging of the story about a girl who falls down a rabbit hole." Eliot switched off his microphone and sent the record in motion. His left hand slid the compact disc equalizer toward zero, dissolving the background music as his right hand simultaneously called forth Waits's incantation. For a single beat the two songs harmonized perfectly, and in that briefest moment conjured Eliot's 100% perfect girl.

Eliot did a double take. The girl with ale-brown hair was lingering outside the studio window, singing along to the background music and curiously listening to Eliot explain the tragedy of Robert Johnson. When she heard Tom Waits intone her name she was compelled to appear within the window's frame and rap on the glass. Her eyes were wonderful, and her smile perplexed. She pointed toward the previously feckless speaker and said, though Eliot could not hear her, "That's me."

Eliot froze like one does when somebody falls down in a crowded, public place and everyone in attendance is momentarily arrested, unsure what to do about the spectacle, embarrassed to have witnessed it. Eliot, who had been thinking all day about disappearance, was stunned by the appearance of Alice Browne.

Her face was a cathedral: noble lips, celestial nose, and eyes the pale blue of a Lou Reed lyric. He was charmed. For all that vanished from the world, here was a different type of magic at work. Where once there was nothing now stood frightening potential, wrapped in a navy-blue pea coat and a mustard-yellow knit cap trimmed with a wooden button. Her subtle fingers splayed upon the glass, perfectly unique. Just before the pause between them grew too thick, Eliot raised his eyebrows and pointed toward the side-door. Alice nodded and disappeared around the corner toward the studio entrance. Tom Waits crooned as Eliot opened the door.

*   *   *

They stood outside the on-air studio sizing one another up. The two of them would make a handsome couple, but neither was entirely certain how to begin the conversation that would eventually pair them in a relationship, successful or otherwise.

Eliot stole a glance at the small tattoo behind her right ear: a thin outline of New York State encompassing three solid black letters: VGN.

Alice Broke the silence, "I'm from Buffalo," she explained, half-embarrassed.

"I'm from here," Eliot offered.

"Go Rustbelt," Alice said and half-heartedly pumped her fist toward the ceiling.

Eliot laughed. "Yeah. So, what brings you down this lonely hall at 2:07 AM on a Saturday morning?"

"I'd say you summoned me," she swayed her shoulders back-and-forth as if she couldn't help but dance to the song that shared her name.

"But I've been working on this incantation for months, why now?" Eliot followed her lead. He was in uncharted territory when it came to talking to women, and Alice seemed comfortable enough to guide them both through this inaugural conversation.

"So, you've been watching me?" She asked, not knowing that he had indeed been watching her.

Eliot felt his face blush. Their sweet story had already begun to sour. "Yeah, but not in a creepy kind of way," he said.

Not realizing there was any truth to Eliot's confession, Alice continued the play, "Well, I've been creepily watching you."

Eliot laughed, "All right."

"Anyway, it's snowing outside, and I've got this tradition of collecting the first flakes of the season. This is number fifteen." She held up her evidence. The white fluff had already begun to melt and compact inside the bell jar.

"I like it," Eliot said. He didn't tell her that he also had a ritual that he performed on the night of each year's first snowfall. He thought it would sound false, as if he were making it up to score points in a game of compatibility they had only just begun to play.

"How about you, do you have any traditions?" Alice asked him.

"Season appropriate?"

"Yeah."

"Well, I guess, I mean, it's stupid, but my dad and I watch *National Lampoon's Christmas Vacation* after dinner every Thanksgiving since I was like ten. I didn't even get the jokes when we first started."

"I've never seen it," Alice said.

"What?! You'll die. It's hilarious. We'll have to watch it." Eliot said. His guts tightened and his sweat glands began pumping. He felt like he had just stepped on a landmine's trigger device and, should he move, the whole station would crumble around him brick by brick.

"It's a date!" Alice said. "But I'll have to take a rain check. I'm heading home for the break."

"Yeah, sure not a problem," Eliot said. His metaphorical explosive device turned out to be a dud. "We actually watch it almost every night between the holidays, so we'll have plenty of opportunities."

"Okay. That's a little intense."

"It's funny is all," he said. Eliot made no mention that on the evening of the season's first snowfall—as dump trucks were filled with salt and outfitted with sharpened plows, and hopeful children huddled around television sets to watch the horrors of the evening news as school-closings skated across the bottom of their screens, and as snow formed a small pillow atop his mother's headstone, and blanketed evergreen wreaths placed lovingly at the foot of grave after grave after grave—he would settle down in the basement of his father's closed bookstore and read James Joyce's "The Dead."

"We'll see," Alice said.

"Oh, you will!" Eliot said. "But that still doesn't explain why you would end up over here in the middle of the night."

"Right. Well, once I got outside I realized I could also use a warm cup of coffee, so I'm actually headed to The Underground. I'm finishing up a paper for my Gothic lit. class so, you know, brain fuel. But then I heard you talking about Faust, so I stopped to listen for a minute."

"And a good thing you did," Eliot said as he disappeared into the On-Air Studio. He came back holding a tall thermos. "You don't want to drink that swill they serve in The Underground. It smells like a rubber fire."

"I just need the caffeine," she said as he motioned for her to hand over her reusable mug.

He shook his head and unscrewed the thermos cap. Steam billowed out of the chrome stack as if from a trans-Atlantic steamer. Eliot poured the coffee and handed the mug back to Alice. She hung her nose over the edge of the rim and smelled dark cherries and toasted hazelnuts. "What is this?" She asked, surprised.

"Coffee," Eliot said.

"Right, but what's in it?" She asked.

"Nothing. That's what good coffee is supposed to smell like," he said.

She brought the mug to her lips and slurped, sizing Eliot up over the rim as he did the same in return. She liked him. He possessed an enviable attention to real-world detail, she observed. Most of her friends were more concerned with cultivating an online persona to keep the dating mill spinning than connecting with one another through the senses. That night, however, she had been seduced by a Tom Waits's lyric and the aroma of Eliot's small gift. She had wanted to touch him, too, to feel with the tips of her fingers the character of Eliot Hopkins. But the song was ending, and she was avoiding landmines of her own. Eliot had vanished, for a second time, into the On-Air Studio. She followed.

"Where did you get this coffee?" Alice asked.

"Gypsy. They're a small roaster in the Gordon Square Arts District."

Alice shook her head.

"It's like a half hour drive from here," Eliot explained the distance in terms of time, which Alice had always thought a thoroughly Midwestern idiosyncrasy.

The coincidence of that evening's events had begun to worry Eliot as the song that had conjured Alice Browne fainted toward its final note. What if this wasn't real? What if he had fallen asleep at the soundboard again? What if —

Her lips touched his cheek. "Thank you for the coffee," she said. "And the song," she added.

"Hey, Alice, I was planning to go to the West Side Market tomorrow. Would you like to come along?" Eliot asked the girl with ale-brown hair. "We could grab some lunch."

"I've never been there," Alice admitted. In her three-and-a-half years at John Carroll she hadn't been west of downtown except to get to the airport. "Do you think they'll have anything for me to eat?"

"They've got all kinds of things to eat," Eliot said.

"Oh, sorry, you asked about my tattoo earlier and when you didn't press about the letters, I figured you knew what they meant," Alice said.

"I do," he said. Eliot thought about heeding Haruki Murakami's advice: *I should tell her that she is the one hundred percent perfect girl for me. No, she wouldn't believe it. Or, 'sorry,' she'd say, 'you're not the one hundred percent perfect boy for me.'* "I figured we could eat at Maha's Falafel Stand."

"I love falafel. We should definitely go!" she said.

"There's a great coffee shop right across the street, too," Eliot added.

"But," Alice stopped him, "we'll go on our one-month anniversary."

"Wait," he said. "What?"

"We'll go one month from today," she insisted. "To celebrate."

"Okay," Eliot said, more than a bit confused. He began to wonder if Alice and her kiss were the result of an unwitting deal with the Devil.

"In the meantime, I'm going to take you to have the best falafel ever!" She said.

"O–kay," Eliot said, even more worried that things just weren't adding up.

"It's at the corner of 31st and 8th." Alice tried to suppress a smile while Eliot worked to locate the intersection in the atlas of his mind. She could wait only a few seconds more before asking him if he had ever been to New York City.

"You want me to go to New York?" He asked. "With you?"

"Oh, the things we'll learn about one another!" Alice said.

A Tour of Cleveland Heights
October 11, 2013

A WEEK LATER, Alice and Eliot set out from her dorm room to walk along the three miles of tree-lined streets and suburban parkland from the JCU campus to Big Sleep Books. It was a pilgrimage of sorts, retracing the route Eliot had walked and biked and driven for longer than she knew that John Carroll University was even a place.

Eliot guided her through the back streets of University Heights along Washington Boulevard, past City Hall and across Cedar Road. He led her through the avenues of his childhood, pointing out the sandlot where he played pickup baseball with his friends from grade school who had all moved away, and the public library where he, too, was able to escape. He had spent the majority of his teenage years in that library reading the big-hearted spinning out of lifetimes by Raymond Carver and Larry Brown, or at the small Cain Park amphitheater listening to local blues musicians proclaim their burning-river bitterness.

"You're an old soul," Alice had observed.

He agreed.

The two strolled, hand-in-hand, along Euclid Heights Boulevard in the direction of Coventry Road when they encountered Cornell walking toward them with Dillinger. The dog was characteristically aloof, his leash hanging slack in his large mouth. Alice had spied the Great Dane before Eliot could say anything, and commented on his magnificence. "Look at that dog!"

Eliot smiled knowingly. The four of them met in front of a deep pile of leaves that had been raked into the street. Cornell slid his headphones from his ears to where they rested around his neck.

"Eliot Ness!" he said to Alice's surprise.

"Alice, this is Cornell," Eliot explained.

"Ah, Miss Alice," Cornell said, stealing a look at Eliot.

"Oh! Nice to meet you," she said. "That means this must be Dillinger?"

"It is," Eliot said. Dillinger rammed his nose into Alice's crotch. "Sorry, he's fairly intrusive."

"Nonsense. That is the Dane's formal greeting. He's merely granting you the courtesy of a royal hello," Cornell corrected Eliot.

"Okay," Alice laughed, taking the dog's large, mushy head in both hands and jostling it back and forth. Dillinger's ears and jowls flopped about noisily.

"Whatcha got?" Eliot said to Cornell.

"Thelonious Monk."

"Which?"

"*Paris 1969.*"

"Play her 'Nutty.'"

"Now don't be rude, Ness. We're having a chat." He turned to Alice, "Would you care for a listen?" Cornell passed his headphones to Alice who took them and put them over her ears. The crowd offered its applause as if they approved of her decision. Monk pounded out a few bars on the keys, inviting Joe Jones's snare into the conversation. Dillinger leaned his body into Alice's left hip, and she rested her hand on his back, patting along with the percussion line.

"How's the old man?" Eliot asked Cornell.

"Pretty good. You two coming by the shop, then?" Cornell asked.

"Yeah, that's the plan."

"Cool, cool. Frank will be happy."

Eliot winked at Alice and joined her in scratching Dillinger's shoulders. Pleased with the attention, the dog attempted to lick Eliot's hand. Prepared for this reaction, he successfully dodged Dillinger's tongue a few times before his persistence paid off. "Eaugh!" Eliot said and wiped a substantial amount of slime and spongy bits of kibble into his jeans. Alice laughed, and the headphones slid from her ears.

"So, where are you two headed?" She asked Cornell.

"Just around the block. I might stop for a cup of mud at Phoenix," he said.

"All right, I think we'll catch up with you at the shop," Eliot said. "Unless you want some coffee," he asked Alice.

"Um. I'm okay, I think. We could swing by later after we meet your dad." She gave Dillinger a final pat against his broadside, and then held out her arms to offer Cornell a hug. "It was nice to meet you, Cornell. I guess we'll see you in a couple minutes?"

"Yes, ma'am," Cornell said. Then, turning to Eliot, "She's dazzling, man."

"Keep it in your pants."

He raised his eyebrows at Alice as if about to pay her a compliment: "I would suggest that you *not* do the same."

She handed him back the headphones. "It was a pleasure to finally lay eyes on you, Miss Alice. I had heard, but the description did not compare." He waved his finger at Eliot.

"Okay," Eliot said, thoroughly embarrassed by his friend's indelicacy. "We'll see you back at Big Sleep." They parted in opposite directions. Cornell looked back, twice. "You'll have to excuse him. He's kind of like a really old big brother."

"Not a problem, Eliot Ness." She joked.

He laughed. "Yeah, that's just one of Cornell's things. Well, my dad's thing, I guess. I'm sort of named after him."

"Really?"

"Yeah, my dad is kind of obsessed with The Untouchables," he said. "And my mom didn't have much say in the matter."

She touched her lips to his as if thanking him for the information.

"What was that for, Sweetest?" Eliot asked.

"Sweetest?" she asked.

"Oh, hmm. It's kind of a Northeast Ohio thing, I guess."

"How so?"

"Have you ever heard of Sweetest Day?" Eliot asked.

"No."

"Well, It's a Cleveland tradition. A 'Hallmark Holiday,' really, though the greeting card company had nothing to do with its inception." Eliot said.

"So it's like a secular Valentines Day?" Alice offered.

"I guess," Eliot conceded, "but hasn't Capitalism already annulled the Saint from Valentine's Day?"

"Smash the patriarchy!"

"Huh?" Eliot asked.

"It's a way for men to buy a woman's love with chocolate, roses, and jewelry. Love is worth more than a handful of junk on a single day."

"Well, then Sweetest Day is no better. It was all a ploy to sell chocolate." A committee of twelve local confectioners had created the candy-selling gimmick in October 1921, the same year that Eliot's great-grandparents arrived in Cleveland. For nearly a century, Rust-belt women had been showering their men with gifts of sweets. Most boys learned of the holiday during their childhoods through gifts they received from their mothers. "I never celebrated it."

"I love you because we hate the same things." Alice said,

"Love?" Eliot asked.

"Yep," Alice admitted. "I love you, Sweetest." The couple's mock moniker would stick like caramel in cheap dental work.

They turned right at Coventry Road and arrived almost instantly at the front entrance to Big Sleep Books. Eliot had not used the front door in some time, and had forgotten that his father replaced the shop's actual address with 221b in homage of Sherlock Holmes's Baker Street apartment number. His hand lingered on the doorknob. The front window display was fairly bare: a handful of recently published paperbacks lined the windowsill terminating at a tall pile of deluxe edition Clue board games. A small poster announcing a book signing from the previous winter still hung in the window. As they walked inside, Eliot ripped the poster down.

"Think we can get rid of this?" He asked Frank, who was reading a Chicago street atlas at the counter.

"Sure, sure," Frank said, quickly stuffing the atlas beneath the counter and crossing his massive forearms across his chest. "I wasn't expecting you just yet."

"I wanted to bring Alice by the shop." She followed him through the door.

"Hi," Alice said.

"Ah! Hello, dear," Frank said, surprised. His eyes softened and his arms relaxed. "It's very nice to meet you."

"Oh, thank you. It's nice to meet you as well. Eliot has told me a lot about you," she said.

Frank raised his eyebrows at his son, who hadn't told him much about the girl standing before him. "He tells me you're a writer," he said. Frank rubbed at his beard to both make sure it was in place and that it held no crumbs.

"I guess that's technically true." Alice was a bit embarrassed by the label, surrounded as she was by all those hefty books: published, bought, read, traded, adopted, loved again. Her mind turned curiously to Anselm Kiefer and *Lot's Wife*, which she had seen on display during each of her almost weekly visits to the Cleveland Museum of Art. His painting was a wasteland of oil and ash, of stucco and chalk, of salt that would evaporate as its wooden panels unfurled over time. Kiefer had transformed the tragedy of death into a process of beautiful decay. His art was temporality illuminated—a melting snowflake, the crash of a wave. The shop's slow-moving inventory seemed more permanent. It weighed on her.

"My wife was a writer," Frank said. Eliot was surprised to hear Frank mention his mother. "It's a good profession, bewitching the world. Got anything in the works?"

"I do," she said. "My Senior Thesis is a creative project. A novel, actually. I'm hoping to finish it up in the next couple of weeks. It's due at the end of this term."

"She's very tight-lipped about the whole thing. I don't even know the title," Eliot prodded.

"You will. I just want it to be right. You'll be the first to read it, I promise," Alice said to Eliot, adding, "Titles are hard."

"Well, what's it about?" Frank tried.

Eliot chuckled, having attempted this most dreaded of questions a few times already to no avail. He ducked behind the counter and tossed the book-signing advertisement into a recycling bin.

Alice leaned upon the railing that led up to the second-floor loft. "Remorse," she said.

"A love story, then?" Frank pressed.

"Aren't they all?" Alice said.

"I'm afraid so," Frank said, and, laying his hand over his heart, winked at her.

Eliot, standing next to his father behind the high-top counter of Big Sleep Books, looked at Alice as if she had just revealed the secret to a complex illusion.

A Tour of Manhattan
October 25, 2013

"ALICE, THIS IS NICK CARAWAY," Eliot said. "Nick, Alice Browne." Nick hugged Alice with all the charm of an old friend.

"Nick Caraway," Alice said to Eliot. "You have a friend named Nick Caraway who moved from the Midwest to New York City?"

"I do," Eliot confirmed with a wry smile.

"Like *Gatsby*." She said. The note of excitement mixed with disbelief in her voice tickled the old friends.

"Only one 'r,'" Nick offered through a practiced chuckle that suggested he was used to this response. "So, less *Gatsby*, more...rye." The pause in his explanation had been perfected over the course of several dozen performances. New Yorkers, he had found, love *Gatsby*. The city itself had never quite recovered from Fitzgerald's portrait.

Eliot clapped his friend on the back and said, "Come on, Old Sport." Nick's face burst into a wide, toothy grin, and he slung his arm around Eliot's neck. They walked out of Grand Central Terminal and onto East 42nd Street. It was unseasonably warm. The sun gleamed against the tips of buildings that cast their shadows upon the sidewalks far, far below. Intersections were alive with light and movement. Eliot looked up, as one does upon entering the outdoors in New York City for the fist time. His antique valise, plastered with luggage decals from semi-exotic locales he had never actually been, knocked against his knee with each step. Nick slung Alice's canvas duffel bag over his shoulder.

Eliot, walking backwards, looked with wonder upon what he thought was the Empire State Building and felt small: a colony of atoms beneath the watchful gaze of titans. He would come to find that this initial impression of the city was, however, false. No one watched, and 'Empire' seemed to mean something completely different in the context of this city. He was comfortably anonymous, like the less famous buildings that played a supporting cast to the better-known landmarks (or like other less fanciful cities altogether; he thought of Cleveland). The anonymity was liberating. He focused the lens of his imagination upon the stories that lay behind all those steel curtains and concrete shutters as if he could salvage the integrity of each individual contribution to this unfamiliar place through attention alone.

"Eyes on the pavement, friend!" Nick said to Eliot as he pulled him back onto the curb from the gutter of Vanderbilt Ave. "There'll be plenty of time for lying in ditches and looking up at the stars once we've located a proper pint." Eliot obediently returned his gaze to street level. He glanced back at Alice, inviting her into their ranks.

To her they looked more like Dean Moriarty and Sal Paradise than Jay Gatsby and Nick Carraway. "So, gentlemen, where to?"

"Well, that depends," Nick said to her, "on how boozy you're feeling."

She didn't miss a beat, "Let's quaff, Old Sport!" The three of them erupted with laughter on their way across 42nd Street toward 5th Avenue. Nick rolled up the sleeves of his faded chambray button down to reveal the beaten face of an old wristwatch.

"One-thirty," he said. "What time are your appointments?"

"Dinner is at eight o'clock," Alice said.

"Whereabouts?" Nick asked.

"The Lillian Vernon Creative Writers House," she said.

"NYU," Eliot said to Nick.

"The West Village it is. Let's ditch these bags on the way," Nick suggested.

The three of them walked along 5th Avenue neglecting, like a five-day-per-week commuter on the Connecticut line, the riches offered by even the briefest detour down any cross street. They passed The Library, an imperial Beaux-Arts building punctuated by a pair of marble lions that Paul Goldberger had once deemed 'New York's most lovable public sculpture,' and then the actual Empire State Building. A string of yellow cabs lined the entire block. They saw their reflections in the plate glass windows of the Heartland Brewery as they elbowed their way against the current of a hustling crowd that didn't abide by walk signals, which therefore elicited horn blasts and derisive stares from the hired drivers of black town cars with embassy license plates.

The Flatiron Building, surrounded by gilded clocks and a paronomasian café, attested to the unique vision of nineteenth-century New York. Still, the 'X' of 5th Avenue and Broadway marked the spot of nothing in particular. The trio continued south along the meridian of 5th Avenue, the streets marked East on their left, West on their right. They paused at the corner of 16th to observe the bustle of Union Square Park, a single block away to the East. Nick rested Alice's duffel atop a pair of graffitied mailboxes while Eliot placed a hand on the construction scaffolding that framed the corner building. Alice hung her toes over the curb.

"Looks like the farmers market is open today. You two interested in taking a peek?" Nick asked. The tourists were both apathetic at best, especially since they could just make out the top of the Washington Square Arch in the distance, as if that were their destination. In a few blocks they would also see the awnings begin to turn mostly purple, indicating that they had arrived on campus (which looked nothing like a campus, according to Eliot). Nick hoisted the duffle atop his shoulder once again. They slogged on, diverting east down West 10th Street to check in at the Lillian Vernon Creative Writers House.

A student worker took their bags to one of the few guest rooms on the third floor reserved for prospective students after confirming their invitation in an over-sized book labeled 'Visitors.' Alice Browne's name was written on a page that looked to be about half way through the life of the tomb. Squeezed between her name and phone number someone had printed '+1.' Alice asked the work-study girl at the desk if she might recommend a bar where writers in the program mingled.

"You could try The Four-Faced Liar," she offered. The way she said it did not insinuate that she had ever been there, nor that she was entirely certain anyone from the program drank there regularly. In fact, her recommendation seemed predicated only upon its proximity to the Creative Writers House. Nonetheless, Nick seconded the suggestion and they were off.

It was a short walk to the unassuming pub. Nick entered first, followed by Alice, and then Eliot. They were all pleased with the warm glow of the yellow light refracted off the tin ceiling. It gave the appearance of a gas-lit era. A clock's reflection set like the sun on the polished bar. "Fairytale of New York" kissed their ears, and danced in the air where once tendrils of dense cigarette smoke would have spun. Nick cozied up to the bar and ordered a round of Manhattans. Ice cubes spilled into glasses with a silvery clatter. Conversations hummed. Alice took stock of the poets and drunks—each indecipherable from the other. A woman in a three-piece, pin-striped suit wearing short-cropped hair and a penciled on mustache took a connoisseur's drag from a deep glass and winked at Nick above the rim. She twirled like a pinwheel on her revolving stool and disappeared into a snug nook with her cocktail. Alice raised the martini glass that the bartender had just sat before her in salute to the woman's audacity. "Well, here we are," she laughed. "Wherever here may be."

"Yes," Eliot said and chirped the rim of his Manhattan against her already raised glass. "So tell us, Nick, what have you been up to?"

Nick joined his cocktail with theirs: "I'm basically a French Carny," he said, and filled his mouth with liquor. Alice and Eliot waited for an explanation. He allowed the drink to coat his mouth, inducing a faint sting before it warmed his throat. Then, contemplating the premature shallowness of his glass, and, before continuing his story, Nick called out to the bartender: "Adrian, another round, please." Alice and Eliot exchanged glances.

Of all the bars in New York City that the desk clerk could have recommended, she had, it seemed to them, suggested a place that Nick frequents on the regular. "So you come here often?" Eliot asked the question he and Alice had both been thinking.

"Where, the Four-Faced Liar?" Nick said, shaking his head and shaping his face into a loose frown. "Never been here before in my life. Nice place, though, and they're generous with the booze."

"But you know the bartender's name," Alice said, confused.

"I do," Nick smiled. To Alice, he seemed more legend than man, like the faceless characters of a Magritte painting who could use their imaginations to will anything they'd like into being. If she had been in a classroom and not a West Village bar, she would have thought of Oscar Wilde: "There is nothing that art cannot express." She contemplated what sort of artist Nick Caraway might be, if he were any sort of artist at all. She wasn't entirely certain that Wilde's expression was true, especially as she worked on completing the final draft of her own novel, which she found didn't express much of anything at all. Alice wondered how Nick and Eliot had become friends, but as she was about to place the question before them, Nick continued: "As with all things, there was a sign. And the sign read, 'Pipe organ recital at St. Thomas's, 5:15pm.' So I went, and some Juilliard cat was blowing the lid off the place. The lesson here," he looked at Eliot, "is that if you see a sign advertising a pipe organ recital, you should go—even if it isn't free. But, I digress."

The man who Nick had called Adrian, and who had not, interestingly enough, corrected him, delivered their drinks. Eliot poured the remainder of his first drink down his throat so as not to accumulate a collection of glasses. The man they called Adrian took Eliot's empty glass with him to the opposite end of the long mahogany bar. "Anyhow," Nick continued, "I sat down near the back of the church next to a man in a top hat. I figured he was part of the production, his dress seemed to match the general tenor of the performance—this was Christmastime last year, mind you—and I wanted to sit close enough to see just what he might get himself up to. In this city you can actively seek out new doors, but one must too often simply wait to see how many of them will open. During intermission he and his friend began chatting about the quality of the wood from which the pews had been carved. I had said something about using a pew-back as a headboard in college, remember that piece we hauled out of the antique shop on Water Street? Next to Cajun Dave's?"

"I do!" Eliot exclaimed, only a touch too excited for the memory that had elicited his outburst.

"Well, I left that thing at Kent, it was too much of a hassle to move out here, but I wouldn't mind finding a replacement. Except, I told Mr. Masclet, that was his name, I wasn't entirely certain where one such as myself would go about acquiring the raw materials so to speak." Nick's story had caught the attention of a few other patrons. Their conversations stalled and they leaned, ever so slightly, toward the trio at the bar.

Alice, taking note of the eavesdroppers, began to realize that she and Eliot and Nick were "misdressed." Underdressed would have been imprecise, she suspected—they were simply dressed wrongly. Shabby tweed jackets hung upon the high backs of chairs, hats perched upon tables next to emptied pint glasses, suspenders slung over boney shoulders, and ties draped around thin necks. The men wore smiles beneath their mustaches, and the women all held flowers in their hair. Alice was beginning to feel as if she had entered an experimental theater production without foreknowledge or ticket. She was unsure how to act, where to look, if anywhere, other than upon the ripples of her drink.

"Turns out, Mr. Masclet did know where one who was so inclined could procure old church pews. As it happened, he had an entire warehouse full of the things back in Paris. When I told him that would be a hell of a long way for me to go to get a headboard, and that I could probably pick one up at the Russian Junk Shop on West 14th, he agreed and asked me if I was from the area, or knew one of the musicians. Anyway, we got to talking a bit more and I learned that he owns one of the largest collections of nineteenth-century carnival equipment in the world, and that he was in New York that winter to finalize plans to bring his collection to Governors Island the following summer. When I asked what that had to do with the old pews, he said that his master builders used them as patch-wood to repair any broken rides or games. Everything in his collection was wooden, including the steam-powered calliope and pedal-operated carousels. Mr. Masclet insisted that I see the exhibit. He reached into his coat and withdrew a business card, which he passed me, reading the script on the front of the card: 'Fête Paradiso.' It was like an incantation. A vision of La Belle Époque flashed in my mind. Intermission had ended, and another student had begun playing the pipe organ; I couldn't help but think of the shaded woods and picturesque sand castles on Governors Island, which, to be honest, I figured looked something like Seurat's 'A Sunday Afternoon on the Island of La Grande Jatte.' I wasn't wrong."

"It sounds great," Eliot said.

"Unfortunately, I had to tell Mr. Masclet that I would be spending the summer in St. Thomas—"

"Yes, because that's unfortunate," Alice said.

"Well-played. But I had been out of work for the better part of the year, so I wasn't exactly going to be living extravagantly down there," Nick said. "I was hoping to pick up a few odd jobs, save up some cash, and eventually make my way back up here in the fall. Plus, the rent's always cheap in the islands."

"His dad has a place," Eliot explained to Alice.

"Anyhow, Mr. Masclet offered me a job as the *Fête* chronicler, so I signed on."

"Chronicler?" Alice asked. "I thought you said you were a carney? Ride operator, weight guesser, that kind of thing."

"I said I'm *basically* a carney. I'm actually in charge of loading and unloading the exhibits and report their condition," he said to Alice. "I take a lot of pictures." Her eyes followed Nick's arm as he pointed with his glass at the bartender, who had sunk into a wicker rocking chair beneath a dim, frosted lamp that spilled forth an ivory-colored light. His own drink sat atop an end-table next to a small, potted holly bush and a rotary telephone. He held open upon his lap a doorstopper of a novel. "Adrian works in the absinthe tent. He's a total chemistry wonk." Nick said. Alice felt cheated, like the moment in one of Anne Radcliffe's Gothic novels when the supernatural elements are explained away to reveal more worldly, rational evidence.

Nick continued demystifying the pub's occupants: "Djuna, I'm not certain that's her real name, but, you know, the girl with the tattooed moustache and bowler hat you saw when we first arrived, is our resident calliope mechanic. Man, she can make that thing howl. It swells inside your gut until you're under its spell and all you can do is dance.

"What's a calliope?" Eliot asked, only now half-listening to the story.

"It's sort of a larger-than-life music box," Nick said. "The whole thing's analog. Steam motorizes a complex pulley system that moves these carved figurines that play drums and bells…and I think one works a squeeze-box. There's also a belt system that spins the roller mechanism for the player-piano punch card wheel—tell you what, you've got to see it! I'll give you a tour when you move down." Nick had been speaking to both of them, moving his eyes between Alice and Eliot, assuming they were certain about Alice's acceptance in the NYU Creative Writing Program, and the big move.

"It all depends on school," Alice said. "We might end up in Iowa…or Wisconsin."

"Wow. What are your safety schools?" Nick said.

"Texas," Alice said.

"You ever read her stuff?" Nick asked without answer. "Her safety school is a top five program."

"Eight," Alice corrected.

"Maybe so, but still. Are you confident?" Nick said.

"My adviser tells me I should be."

"Modesty. Every writer I know thinks their stuff is terrible. Mostly it is. But what better place to write bad prose than New York City?" Nick asked.

"Exactly," Alice said.

"It's too bad you two won't be here next week. A group of us is going to Candle 79 and then to see *Sleep No More* on Halloween night."

"Oh, that would have been fun!" Alice said.

"I don't know what that is," Eliot admitted.

"Well, we could grab some lunch there tomorrow before you head out if you don't have any plans," Nick suggested without explanation to Eliot.

"We actually have reservations for falafel at 31st and 8th," Alice said.

Nick thought for a moment, "That's Madison Square Garden."

"That's the falafel truck outside Madison Square Garden," she corrected.

"Well, I guess we'll save the fine dining for when you settle into your posh graduate student housing," Nick said. "If you're looking for work,' he said to Eliot, who had gone silent during their exchange, "I might be able to get you something semi-permanent on the *Fête* crew. It would be a blast to work together again, wouldn't it?"

"Definitely," Eliot said, hoping neither Nick nor Alice would detect his lack of enthusiasm. He searched his reflection in the corroded silver of the antique mercury-coated mirror behind the bar, unsure, even, of what he was searching for. Eliot had bolstered his weight upon his boney elbows, which had begun to ache and widen, sinking his shoulders six inches closer to the bar. He looked so old. Not geriatric, but a few years (maybe a decade) closer to the grave than he thought he should appear. His hair, definitively parted along the right side of his scalp and swept left across his head looked like a cowlicked, dark-water tsunami. He ran his fingers through it, and they came away greasy with pomade. He wiped them clean upon his denimed thigh, adjusted his glasses and took a mouthful of alcohol. He was handsomely drunk. Eliot's eyelids dipped, and before they landed, he saw Joseph Kowalski staring back at him from the depths of the foggy, century-old mirror.

"Hey, you two want to grab a coffee and then head over to The Strand?" Nick asked.

"What's that?" Eliot asked.

"Bookstore. Massive!" Nick said.

"That sounds good," Eliot said, perking up. "I could definitely use a cup of caffeine. Anything good close by?"

"Third Rail makes a swell cappuccino. They're down on Sullivan Street, maybe two blocks away."

"Perfect. Let's do it," Eliot said. "Sound good to you?" He asked Alice.

"Absolutely. I was starting to feel the draw of the whiskey's siren song myself," she said.

They settled their tab with Adrian and exited the bar with about an hour of sunlight remaining in the sky. The air had gotten colder, but it wasn't yet the sort of cold that made your skin burn, Eliot thought, the kind brought about by darkness and the winds of change.

At Third Rail, he and Alice purchased matching coffee tumblers, his was filled with an almond milk cappuccino, a tulip poured into the foam, hers with a French Press of a single-origin Nicaraguan coffee. Nick ordered an Americano. They then walked around the emptied Washington Square Park Fountain, craned their necks to marvel at the arch, and paused long enough to toss a few dollars into the lone busker's open cello case.

"I wonder how we'll see the city differently once it's home," Alice said to Eliot, her mouth almost on his ear, her reddened cheeks puffed into a smile.

"What do you mean?" Eliot asked, though he had been thinking something similar.

"Just that I wonder if New Yorkers ever get bored by the splendor of the city. Does this," she pointed to the arch and the musician, "become background noise?"

"Hey Nick," Eliot called back to his friend who had stopped a few paces away to remove the top of his coffee, freeing a plume of steam. "Are you not impressed?" Eliot's arm paralleled Alice's as they both pointed upwards into the arrant sky at the arch.

"Aren't you?" Nick returned with an air of disbelief. The cloud of his question mingled with the coffee's breath in the space above his head.

"Sure, but this is the first time we're seeing it. I mean, how many landmarks do you pass by every day without actually noticing them?"

Nick seriously considered the accusation and begrudgingly admitted, "Quite a few, I'm sure. How many do you pass by?"

"Far fewer," he said. Eliot thought about the afternoons he would spend reading in Graselli Library, looking over the tops of the Georgian homes of University Heights, and the days that he could see clear downtown to make out the shape of the Terminal Tower between clouds smeared thin like chalk erasures. Once the fourth tallest building in the world, it now stood as a reminder of Cleveland's more promising past. "But I do try to find some kind of wonder in them."

"Landmarks are places haunted by significance," said Alice, more to herself than either of the boys in particular. Nick nodded in agreement, and Eliot waited to see if she was making conversation or mental notes for a future story. Looking up at the arch through its embedded spotlights that set fire to the night sky, and listening to the cellist play a melody that set fire to her heart, Alice came to the conclusion that despite its impressive enormity, she preferred private memorials to grand public gestures: a heart-carved tree trunk, the site of a first kiss, a family home.

The three friends exited the park at Waverly Place, which they followed a few blocks east until turning north on Broadway, when, unbeknownst to any of the them, they began to follow the exact course pioneered by Eliot's great-grandfather, Yuri Zupančič, who had walked along that vast avenue from Battery Park to Grand Central Station in 1912. A great deal had changed; a great deal hadn't. The immensity of the New York City skyline still weighed heavy on the dreams of the people who scurried beneath it, but the ravages of Capitalism had cheapened the integrity of façades and dreams alike.

November

Anniversary
November 4, 2013

ALICE BROWNE asked Eliot Hopkins, her boyfriend of one month, if he would accompany her to a mid-morning English class prior to their anniversary lunch date. Eliot had never actually been inside of a college classroom. He often told his few acquaintances at work, and even tried to convince himself, that this was because he refused to pay tuition for the opportunity to sit around with twelve strangers who didn't really want to be there in the first place. And who, therefore, put more effort in trying to remain silent for the entirety of a seventy-five minute meeting twice per week than doing their work. The truth of the matter was simply that his summer job had turned into full-time work, and he found it impossible to escape from the routine and the paycheck. Plus, he reasoned, his dad didn't go to college, and things worked out for him, mostly.

After high school, Eliot found himself in the necessary position of not only working at his dad's bookstore in the evenings, but also working construction nine-to-five to help ensure that the shop, his inheritance, would remain open: Eliot paid the utilities and kicked in a few hundred bucks for the rent every so often. Cornell, who functioned as something of an older brother or hip uncle, had implored him on a number of occasions to at least take some evening classes, but argued that he had a library card and that was good enough. But, when Alice invited him to class, he found himself rather curious to see first hand if his assumptions about the ivory tower were correct: that the university is a place that tears people from their homes and turns them into rootless commodities. Who could blame them for their lack of curiosity and excitement— two virtues Eliot had developed while reading old paperbacks in the cab of a construction truck during his coffee breaks.

The two of them walked along the west end of John Carroll's residential quad. Eliot slung his arm over her shoulder. His shoes, a graying pair of once-black Chucks, ground the crisp, auburn leaves beneath his feet into a fine spice that swirled across the concrete walk. The sun shone bright in the baby-blue sky, but offered no heat. Alice wrapped her arm around Eliot's waist, holding him close.

"I kind of can't believe you agreed to come with me," Alice said, her breath visible.

"Why not? The class sounds really interesting."

"I just know that you hate how people can get when talking about lit-er-a-ture." Alice articulated all four syllables of the word in mock pretentiousness.

"We watched a television show for homework. It's hardly lit-er-a-ture," he echoed.

"I guess that's true."

"And I don't even so much mind pretention, I just hope they're not completely apathetic. What better way to spend an hour than talking about stories?"

"Well, to be fair, the stakes are a bit higher than when you and Cornell debate the likelihood of a zombie apocalypse."

Eliot shrugged. "I guess, but shouldn't you all be geeking out over this stuff? Maybe I've imagined a scenario based solely on movies in which college is all just a little bit too serious, like everyone is too smart to have feelings. What's the point, you know?"

"What movies are you watching?!"

"I don't know," Eliot said, "*With Honors, Mona Lisa Smile, Rudy.*"

"We need to update your catalog to include some truer representations. Haven't you seen *Animal House?*" Alice said.

Eliot laughed.

"I need to understand how people read if I want to be a successful writer, right?" Alice asked.

"I don't know. Kurt Vonnegut studied chemistry," he said.

"I thought he majored in anthropology."

"That too."

"You should really think about taking some classes," Alice said, "Or at least work at the bookstore full time. You're too smart for construction." She retrieved a stick of lip balm from among the contents of her bag that included Eliot's copy of Flannery O'Conner's *Complete Stories*, which they had been taking turns reading to one another. She applied a thin layer of the gloss to her lips and tucked the tube back into her bag before unscrewing the lid of her coffee tumbler, a souvenir from their recent trip to New York City.

"I don't think college students are any smarter than construction workers. Or that somehow a life of the mind is more fulfilling than working with your hands," Eliot said.

"That's not what I meant—"

"Take my dad for example—"

"He does something that he loves for a living. That's all I'm saying. You should open a coffee shop or something," Alice suggested.

"I'm just glad we get to spend the day together," Eliot said, changing the subject. He squeezed her shoulder and touched his lips to the lighter strands of hair poking out from beneath her mustard-yellow hat at the soft corner of her forehead.

Eliot thought about what might have been lost had he not broadcast his thoughts about Robert Johnson's alleged dealings with the Devil one month ago. Or if he hadn't followed up with the unlikely selection of Tom Waits's "Alice"—not even a traditional blues song, just a tune that he had wanted to hear at the time. It was as if the universe had some message to communicate, some secret language intended only for the girl with ale-brown hair who he could not have even hoped to be listening.

"Me, too!" She conceded. "I would have missed you this morning." Alice then pointed to a lone figure she had spotted walking in circles around the cobblestone terrace of Rodman Hall.

Eliot knew that the man was walking the labyrinth, a replica of the sacred maze laid in the floor of the Notre Dame Cathedral at Chartres. Eliot had once walked it a week or so after they had originally installed it a few years prior. The loud snap of fabric high above his head grabbed his attention. He swung his head away from Rodman Hall to look at the flag blowing sharply against the wind atop its pole at the center of the quad. His gaze followed the pole down to the ground where, at its base, four Adirondack chairs formed a tight circle around a small mountain of tall silver cans reflecting the sun and the previous evening's merriment. *What movies am I watching?* "Do you ever think about all the people we literally miss every day?" He asked Alice. "Not so much the billions of people spread across the world in places we'll never even visit, but the ones who live at the edges of our own lives?"

"Not really. I mean, I guess not. I tend to pay attention to the people who are important to me." She offered him a smile to indicate that she meant him. "Why, what are you getting at?"

"Nothing, really." Eliot wondered if he was more sensitive to the ghosts haunting the fringe of his reality because he had been touched by death prior to experiencing a single pleasure of human life. "It just struck me that we would have completely missed each other if it hadn't bizarrely snowed in early October this year, and if you didn't have a fourteen-year-old tradition of collecting the first snowfall of the season, and then decided to get a cup of coffee from The Underground at the exact time I was playing a song that shares your name. Not to mention all the luck of our parents meeting and falling in love and having children…and their parents' parents and so on. It's kind of—"

"Magic."

"Well, yeah." He sucked a droplet of snot that had been dangling from his left nostril, then audibly slurped coffee from his own coffee mug. "And it all unbelievably took place…here."

"Cleveland city of light, city of magic," Alice sang.

"You do that a lot, you know?" Eliot said.

"What?"

"Quote songs to prove a point." He didn't mind, really. In fact, he found it kind of endearing, as if there was nothing that art could not express.

"Cleveland city of light, you're calling me," she continued. Then asked, "So, you know this one?"

"Randy Newman. *Major League*," he confirmed. "Any Clevelander worth their Ball Park Mustard knows *that* one." They had reached the oversized bronze bust of John Carroll and turned right toward the O'Malley Center where they could see three of Alice's classmates release the final plumes of cigarette smoke into the frigid air before dropping their still smoldering butts to the ground and disappearing into the building.

The couple arrived at the entrance where the heavy door had just completed it's lethargic close only to be yanked open once again for them to enter the stairwell behind the trio of smokers. Their stench lingered at the bottom of the stairs to mix with the lemon-scented cleaner while their heavy footfalls echoed down from above. Eliot removed his glasses and wiped the fog from the lenses with the hem of his sweater as Alice's boots added a steady *clap* to the irregular thuds and thumps of people climbing and descending the stairs.

They were a few minutes early. The room was overly lit by the obnoxious intensity of fluorescent light reflecting off lily-white walls. Eleven students and Eliot sat around a large, modular conference table. The gloss of the table's blue and gray veneer provided the light with another surface off of which to deflect—the glare gave Eliot a slight headache. The bare walls amplified the small sound of each student's pre-class rituals. Someone cleared his throat and it sounded to Eliot like a hoard of growling zombies. He sat as still as possible, feeling hopelessly out of place. No books piled in front of him. He had brought only a small, pocket-sized notebook and a blue pen, which sat before him next to his coffee mug, now empty. He looked at Alice for some sense of what to do, but she was intent upon the notes she had scrawled in her own notebook. A few of the other students' eyes flitted from their smartphones to Eliot and back, curiously. Eliot's watched beeped to signal the top of the hour, and he felt a hot blush overcome his face. He quickly smashed the small button that would stifle the alert. He could think only of escape.

Professor Amisi Mubarak entered the room. Her heavy Egyptian accent projected an authoritative kindness. Her hair was a wild frizz, and she wore a long, black skirt with a smart cashmere sweater and patent-leather oxfords. She began speaking: "In the era of the French Revolution, the British literary tradition became obsessed with, and haunted by, social change. To engage with and illuminate the Empire's particular breed of historical unrest, British writers turned to evocations of vampires, evil priests, and predatory rebels to express their fears—in other words, they turned to the Gothic." Lapis Lazuli earrings added to her mystique. She reminded Eliot of Alice: keen and unafraid. Alice was Byzantine in her attention to detail. Like any great artist, she could find beauty and wonder in the most improbable things: an overflowing trash can, carpet stains, and even Eliot Hopkins.

Eliot followed the conversation with interest, though he did not contribute. His thoughts kept returning to the previous evening when he and Alice had watched the assigned episode of *Twin Peaks* for that day's class in the dark of her dorm room. They both ended up falling asleep, wrapped in a heavy comforter. Eliot's face pressed against the sweet smell of the pillow he had borrowed from Alice's roommate, Kate. He unintentionally dreamed of its owner.

Saccharine Vexed
April 22, 1978

ELIOT'S MOTHER, Olivia Zupančič, grew up in the house next door to his father, Frank Hopkins, on Lakeshore Boulevard in Euclid, Ohio. They were both enjoying a long-weekend break from their respective first-grade classrooms at Holy Cross Elementary School when their eyes met across the vast expanse of shared suburban backyard. She was looking at pictures from Alice's adventures in Wonderland, and he was swatting baseballs from atop a rubber tee. The knell of his aluminum bat against the hard innards of the ball tolled like a church bell. Olivia raised her eyes above the illustrated cover of her book to peer at Frank, who was charting the arc of the ball like a major leaguer watching his home run disappear beyond the outfield fence. He noticed her in the crowd of birdbaths, garden hoses, and potted plants and their lives grew together like a pair of inosculated beech trees.

When they reached the fourth grade, Frank told Olivia that he was going to be the pope, and also that he planned to play center field for the Cleveland Indians. She believed him; Frank had a smile like the Cheshire Cat. The two of them played together daily. Their favorite routine involved acting out scenes from Olivia's storybooks within the branches of a colossal weeping willow tree that grew at the border of their two yards. Within the confines of the tree they planned their future together as if Frank's unlikely dreams had no bearing on their ability to be married and move to Cedar Point, the amusement park Olivia had visited with her grandparents the previous summer, and which she described to Frank in detail for the entirety of the following year. Olivia's parents, John and Madeline, would watch from the kitchen window, coffee and the Sunday *Plain Dealer* in hand, as the children followed the muddy path churned by years of travel between their homes before disappearing into the cover of the tree's dense foliage.

Once behind the willow's curtain, Frank and Olivia would find themselves in any number of faraway, enchanted realms: The Emerald City, Never Never Land, or The Hundred Acre Wood. Olivia always played the swashbuckling heroine. Her favorite thing to do was to grasp hold of a bunch of willow shoots, test their strength with a sharp tug, and swing from the lower branches in a swooping arc; and, upon landing, to smell the sweet pulp of the leaves that had become jam in her palms. It was akin to the happy scent of a freshly mown lawn, the kind that made her think of lying in the plush, uniform grass of a mid-summer's evening watching fireworks light up the star-spangled sky.

In their teenage years she and Frank would watch those same fireworks from the bow of her grandparent's boat upon the placid waters of Lake Erie's North Coast Harbor. The display's reflection in the glass windows of the Cleveland skyline, and upon the shimmering surface of the lake, was spectacular. As the fierce bursts echoed off the buildings, stealing her breath, she would cradled Frank's hand in hers and imagine the swaddle of their backyard.

A length of nautical rope purchased by her father from the Samsel Supply Company in the Flats, and originally used to secure a tire swing to a low-hanging branch, was used to bind Frank to the willow tree's trunk. She secured him with a stevedore's knot, which she had learned to tie under the guidance of her grandfather, Yuri, who had worked the iron mines in Minnesota, she would tell Frank while pinning him to the tree. His captivity was no doubt ordered by the likes of

Lewis Carroll's Queen of Hearts. A were formidable test of Olivia's bravery among the branches. She would climb to heights that Frank would not dare in order to retrieve the imaginary sacred object necessary to free him from his bonds. Their roles did not drastically change when they graduated from Holy Cross—she to the Villa Angela Academy, and he to St. Joseph's High School—but the plot thickened.

In the tenth grade, a decade after they had fallen in love, their bodies trembled then grooved. They explored each other with scientific precision and naïve fascination. Frank brushed the back of his fingers across the prickly stubble of Olivia's armpits. She delighted in the thrill that tensed her skin, and did not pull away. He discovered a curious mole protruding from her scalp that had been hiding beneath her hair, and wondered what other secrets she had been keeping from him. Olivia's forefinger plumbed the well of Frank's navel. He objected. She felt a pang of jealousy because her own belly button did not so much protrude as sit flush with the surface of her abdominal muscles, which she did not find particularly attractive. She also thought it was funny how each of his toes perfectly nestled against its neighbor. Her toes did not touch one another; neither did her knees.

Their lives held all the promise of quaking mattresses. Olivia had been writing short stories, and publishing them in her high school's literary magazine. In the fall of their senior year, she was accepted on early admission to the creative writing programs at both Hamilton College and Brown University. Frank was courted by a number of schools offering handsome baseball scholarships—most notably the Kenyon College coach had personally called to invite him to play on the team, apologizing that Kenyon only offered academic scholarships, and Frank's grades, while okay, simply didn't make the cut. The Hopkins's couldn't afford the $20,000 per-year price tag, and anyway, Frank and Olivia's heartstrings proved inelastic. They wanted nothing more out of life than one another. Their roots, it seemed, had grown too deep, too interdependent. They had become one without the social glue of marriage or religious ceremony, though the pageantry of those things would follow.

In late-November of that year, before either of them had consciously made the decision not to leave the other, Olivia became couch ridden for nearly a week with that season's unique strand of influenza. Mostly she watched game shows and unending broadcasts of *A Christmas Story* with the rapt attention afforded to one under the spell of a fever and mild dehydration. When the virus struck she had been reading James Joyce's *Ulysses* and was finally nearing its conclusion. To abandon the book, even temporarily, in the middle of Molly's soliloquy was unbearably frustrating, so she asked Frank to skip voluntary after-school conditioning to read to her aloud. He did. Olivia, tired and worn, stretched the length of her parents' couch. Covered in blankets and Saltine dust, she slipped her clammy hand from beneath the frayed Afghan blanket and interlaced her thin fingers with Frank's—the branches of their lives. Frank sat on the floor. His shoulder impressed a crater into the side of the plaid couch and his face pulled close to Olivia's ear. Recklessly, he took a sip of her ginger ale and read to her the remaining lines of the book: "…and then I asked him with my eyes to ask again yes and then he asked me would I yes to say yes my mountain flower and first I put my arms around him yes and drew him down to me so he could feel my breasts all perfume yes and his heart was going like mad and yes I said yes I will Yes."

"Yes, I will," Olivia echoed, "Yes." She twisted a ring from her finger and slid it to the knuckle of Frank's pinky. He looked down at the golden band that had been a gift from Yuri to Muriel on their fiftieth wedding anniversary, and which Yuri had passed on to his granddaughter, Olivia, on her sixteenth birthday. Two days later he joined Muriel in their shared plot at Lake View Cemetery.

After a stuttered instant, no longer than the intended drag between the end of one sentence and the beginning of the next, Frank rubbed the side of his nose against Olivia's smooth cheek and breathed her in. She smelled like a memory: like grass and sulfur and tanning oil, the accumulation of summer. Olivia closed her tired eyes and wound up her lips in a contended smile at Frank's silent acceptance of her proposal. She fell asleep imagining the family she and Frank would make together, and all the small pleasures of growing old with one another.

Frank had carefully planned his proposal, but something about the way in which Olivia unexpectedly took over the process of legally binding their two lives seemed both correct and necessary. Neither of them had actually asked the other to marry. And yet, wondrously, Eliot's parents became engaged in the space between two moments that are all too often taken granted: that of reading a story and that of having finished it. The magic of such moments lasts less than the amount of time it takes a pitcher to deliver a fastball to his catcher's glove, and often goes as unnoticed as a ball, unstruck, high and outside. Frank wondered if it was chance or predestination (both equal possibilities, he guessed) that had prompted Olivia to slide her ring, the color of a million opportunities, upon his finger. He looked at his bride-to-be and recalled the casual chance that had persuaded their lives to intersect at the tolling of bat against ball.

Frank had already reserved a room at The Inn at Cooperstown for a long weekend during their upcoming Christmas Break. The off-season package deal included admission to the National Baseball Hall of Fame and Museum and a tour of the snow-covered Doubleday Field, where Frank planned to crouch behind home plate, a material synecdoche of all he found right and beautiful about the world, and ask Olivia to marry him. They would celebrate with dinner at the

Fly Creek Cider Mill followed by a private tour of the Fenimore Art Museum. But this was better, more honest, a truer reflection of what it means to love and to be loved. Frank felt the feverish warmth of his sleeping fiancé. That new word had already begun to subtly transform their lives with all the charm of an origami crane emerging from a crisp sheet of plain, white paper. He smelled the sweet ginger of her breath, and refused to think of life as being lived only in the brilliant flashes that punctuate the great war of an otherwise banal existence. Life's real beauty, he thought, resides in the everyday miracle of far-reaching serendipity: the deep, awful patterns of dumb luck that had brought them together in the first place, and of which neither of them had the least bit of control.

He set Olivia's copy of *Ulysses* on the end table next to her just-in-case vomit bag and the nearly empty can of Canada Dry ginger ale. She held tight to his hand, even in her sleep, so he settled in and curiously picked up the other paperback lying face down on the table and began to thumb through the pages. It was her father's copy of Raymond Chandler's *The Big Sleep*.

Frank and Olivia were married the summer following graduation. Their friends were surprised that they had both passed up opportunities that would deliver them from Cleveland. Frank's father had even sat him down to ask that he consider what he was passing up: "A chance to play baseball in the bigs! Possibly for money, for Chrissake!" Olivia's mother was likewise concerned for her daughter: "There's more to life than weddings and babies and death, Olive. You're so talented." Her head shook back and forth as if she were speaking from experience. Were it chance that brought them together, it was surely destiny that had wed them. That August, even their high schools were slated to merge, and at the wedding reception Olivia's father, happily drunk on scotch and soda, announced that their union had brought the schools together. Acceptance letters and scholarship offers became memories as irretrievable as drops of rain upon the great lake. New papers arrived: electric bills, credit-card statements, a mortgage.

The newlyweds bought a modest home on Nicholas Avenue behind the Euclid Fire Department where Frank had been hired to put his athletic ability to good use. It was a small house, but ideally located. Frank could hop the fence to work and, more importantly, could make it home to have lunch with his wife. The house had a detached, one-car garage where they parked Frank's wood-paneled 1984 Chrysler LeBaron. Olivia took over as the car's exclusive driver, and appreciated that she didn't have to brush snow from the windshield before heading to work at the preschool where she was a teacher's aid. In the evenings she took writing classes at Cleveland State University or worked from home in the spare bedroom that she painted yellow. She installed a purple orchid upon the windowsill next to a home-run baseball Frank caught off the bat of Candy Maldonado at the Municipal Stadium, and which he handed to Olivia with a kiss that was broadcasted over the jumbotron. Floor-to-ceiling bookshelves and an antique roll-top desk declared in no uncertain terms that it was the office of an aspiring writer. Olivia shifted focus from literary fiction to writing and illustrating children's books. Her most successful title was a self-published detective story about an anthropomorphized foxhound named MacGuffin who specializes in finding lost cats advertised by homemade posters stapled to telephone poles. MacGuffin, ever compassionate, is known for returning the cats to their families without accepting the promised reward.

In late November, 1990, without any pomp or circumstance, Olivia sat on the toilet of the small home's only bathroom, with her jeans crinkled about her ankles and lithe body slumped at the waist, elbows digging into her knees, staring at a vague pink plus sign that was in the process of materializing on the plastic stick she had just peed on. "I'm going to be a mom," she said aloud to no one but herself. "Mom," She repeated.

Frank had been at work since seven o'clock the night before and wasn't due home for another couple of hours. Olivia sat upright and gazed at her navel, flat and unaltered, talking to their baby, "Who are you little one?" She asked. Before leaving the solemn bathroom, Olivia asked her God to watch over the unborn baby, but said nothing of herself.

An instant later she was rushing down the stairs, her hand just barely gliding across the top of the handrail so as not to create too much friction. At the bottom of the steps she rushed past her keys resting within arms reach atop the kitchen table, threw open the back door and skipped into the backyard. Her bare feet, still cold from the bathroom tile, required no time to adjust to the frosted ground, which she was halfway across before realizing she hadn't closed the door. Without hesitation she continued on toward the Fire Station to tell Frank and the guys her good news.

Olivia burst through the side entrance and immediately caught her husband's eye across the room. He was squatting like a catcher behind home plate recording the oxygen levels of each man's long yellow air tank in a notebook the size and shape of a family bible. She held the urine-soaked home pregnancy test above her head in a clenched fist, like so many sacred objects of the past that would have freed a slightly-younger Frank from his willow-shoot bonds, and beamed. He leapt from his work, rushed across the room, and scooped Olivia into his arms. "It's a boy!" He yelled to everyone in the Firehouse, "I just know it's gonna be a boy!" The station erupted in whistles and whoops, hand-clapping and back-slapping. Frank's wish would come true, but at a tremendous price. He would wonder for the rest of his life if in that moment of jubilation he had unknowingly signed some sort of verbal pact with the Devil.

Eliot Hopkins was born seven months later on what would have been his great-grandfather's ninety-sixth birthday: July 8, 1991.

Anniversary
November 4, 2013

AFTER CLASS, to Eliot's surprise, Alice asked if they could visit his mother's grave. Alice set her elbow atop the roof of her fairly new, gun-metal gray Volkswagen GTI, her booted right foot already kicked through the door and resting on the salt-stained floor mat. "Can I meet your mom today?"

Eliot, about to duck into the car through the passenger-side door paused to look at her from across the roof. The sun's rays bathed her face in shimmering phosphorescence. It was far more beautiful than the artificial light of the classroom, and he was happy to have to squint against it. Eliot could see between two of the sun's almost blinding rays only her parted, mulberry-colored lips—disembodied, ethereal. The feeling of want that he experienced as he searched for the rest of Alice Browne behind the sun's flare was as undeniable as any reality he had ever known. She looked divine, and he wanted, not for the last time, to believe.

"I guess." Eliot worked to puzzle out a reasonable explanation as to why she might want to visit his mother's grave in Lake View Cemetery, a spot he had been to only a handful of times himself. His mind hadn't yet fully emerged from Dr. Mubarak's classroom, and was therefore still over analyzing every bit of conversation. Unable to form a direct response to her question, Eliot finally said, "You can't actually see the lake from there, you know."

"I know," she lied, "but the leaves haven't completely fallen, and the sun's out, and I've never been."

"Being in a graveyard is like being in a sanatorium without the threat of conversation."

"Everyone says it's beautiful. I imagine visiting is like receiving a postcard from a deceased loved one, a place where the imagination can confuse the boundaries between past and present," Alice said.

"An imagination afflicted with the disease of nostalgia, yes," he confirmed.

Alice frowned at him. "We don't have to go."

"No. Let's go," he decided. "I just wanted to celebrate us today. That's all. But, you're right. It is one of the prettier Cleveland landmarks. And we might as well take advantage of the sunshine. We might not see it again until May." She was right about the day's charm, he reasoned. And the cemetery, something of an outdoor museum with its chapels and monuments and manicured gardens, was as much a celebration of life as a record of Cleveland's ghosts: John D. Rockefeller, James A. Garfield, Harvey Pekar, Eliot Ness, Olivia Hopkins. He felt a pang in his gut. It might have been the apprehension of introducing Alice to his dead mother. It might, also, have been hunger.

Alice smiled, pulling her lips slightly apart and tugging the corners of her eyes toward a squint. She had already met Eliot's father shortly after the two began dating. Since then, she had been slowly building the story of Eliot Hopkins. And so at every opportunity she liked to visit the curiosity shops and great cathedrals of his past to help pollinate her affection. But understanding Eliot's ghosts was a lot like collecting snowflakes in a bell jar, a practice she had maintained since she was six years old, when she first gathered the inaugural dust of a pitiless Buffalo winter. Fourteen jars of melted snow, each labeled and arranged chronologically from 1998–2012, lined the bookshelves in her bedroom at her parents' house in Upstate New York. The fifteenth currently set upon her desk in Campion Hall, having been collected on the night she had first met Eliot Hopkins in October.

The two situated themselves in Alice's car. Eliot slouched in the passenger seat scrolling through his iPhone for a cemetery-appropriate soundtrack. "What do you want to hear?" He asked.

"Anything. Something fun," she said.

He screwed up his face and thought, *what's fun?* He flicked his thumb against the glass screen a few more times before tapping it once to select a track. Alice had started backing out of the parking space when Bonnie Prince Billy's "Cursed Sleep" began to sing sweetly from the car's speakers.

"This is a pretty song," Alice observed after a few measures. "I wouldn't necessarily say it's fun, though."

"We are going to a cemetery," Eliot pointed out. "You want me to change it?"

"No, I like it. It's kind of a wintery lullaby." Alice drove with both hands on the wheel, releasing her right hand from two o'clock only to shift gears, which Eliot found heartbreakingly adorable.

The song worked at his emotions like no book had done in years, and the sad beauty of its story blended with the melancholy strum of the acoustic guitar nearly watered his eyes. Perhaps, though, he was trying too hard. Eliot had been actively seeking a book, or song, or anything that could make him cry. He wanted to feel something other than unmoored, and sadness seemed the most cathartic emotion.

The November sun amplified through the passenger-side window, warming the right side of his face. Eliot was hot and sleepy. He began to feel not well as they passed through the cemetery gates and onto the labyrinthine roads that wound them past the glass Visitors Center, the Garfield Monument, and the Wade Chapel before bisecting the ponds where the ashes of Eliot Ness had been scattered in 1957. He finally directed Alice to pull off to the right side of the road beneath a cluster of leafless trees.

"She's just up there a ways," Eliot motioned.

"Are you sure you're okay?" Alice asked. She felt a twinge of remorse for having forced him there.

"I'm fine. Cemeteries in general just kind of bum me out. It's not this one in particular," he said. Eliot looked at Alice to reassure her, and then out the car's windshield. "It is rather pretty here. And, actually, it's a shame there's no snow. There's something peaceful about the weight of it all." He opened the door and let a rush of cold wind into the car. The initial blast refreshed him. "Let's go," he said and got out of the car.

They walked together along a shale path. Eliot delighted in the sound that the small stones made beneath the pestle of his feet while Alice scanned the names on nearby gravestones; lists of anonymous names always captured her interest as a would-be novelist. Some of the markers had been so badly eroded that she couldn't make out any letters or numbers, just faint impressions that where there once was life now there was not. The erasure seemed cruel, as if the natural world had annulled from it another inconsequential story. Behind one faded marker Alice spied the looming spire of President James A. Garfield's Monument. The sandstone terrace rested just below the tree line. A round tower, its stone almost black, jutted up from behind the trees. She could see clearly a bank of stained-glass windows framed by wheat-colored limestone that was separated from the shale steeple by a band of oxidized copper coping. At its peak stood what looked to be a cross or a *fleur-de-lys*, she couldn't tell. Some ornament of grandeur. Looking at the monument Alice thought of the early Gothic novels she had been reading for the past two months. The monument oppressed the simpler headstones below it, and made plain the inescapable distinction between those ghosts we invite to haunt us, and those who are not important enough to haunt at all.

"I wonder what this one did to deserve anonymity," Alice said to Eliot.

"Nothing," he said. "It's the way of the world. And this place, this testament to our inevitable reality, serves only to remind us that there's nothing more. Nothing less cold, less final. The real miracle of life is the very thing that most of us refuse to acknowledge: that we are all anonymous." The cold had begun to burn his face, and the tips of his fingers ached. "Even your Garfields and Rockefellers. So high, those pillars of fame that we can see rise above the trees. Their stones, too, will one day vanish, and with them the memory of the people they eulogize, as if they never existed in the first place."

Alice held tight to Eliot's hand, afraid to let him disappear into the cheerless oblivion he described. She didn't know what to say, and so she continued to watch as the ground passed beneath their feet.

"But that's what makes life so enchanting," he continued, squeezing the anchor of her hand. "Don't you think? Our lives, no matter how seemingly trite, are perfectly unique. We don't have to be oil tycoons or Presidents, we just have to live so that someone wants to remember that we once were." Alice realized in that moment the reason Eliot did not often visit his mother's grave. It was because he had no memories of her that were his own—not a sound or a smell or a touch that he could call forth in the glow of a bookstore basement as he willed a connection to her ghost through an Irish story that wasn't about either one of them in particular, but more generally the scripture of remembrance.

Eliot stopped and Alice took an extra step before his hand pulled her back to his side. "Ray Chapman," he said.

"Who?" Alice asked. She thought for a moment that they had arrived at his mother's resting place. She tucked her face behind her scarf, and hugged Eliot tight. She read the gravestone before her: Raymond Johnson Chapmen. Above his name was carved a simple cross; below it, the years 1891 and 1920. "Twenty nine," She said. "The headstone looks new."

"He played shortstop for the Indians," Eliot said. "He's the only player to have died from being hit by a pitch. In fact, his death was at least partially responsible for the infamous spitball ban in 1920."

"How do you even know that?" She asked.

Eliot enjoyed her surprise at his ability to recall mundane facts, but knew that he was not interesting enough to arrange those facts into something enchanting the way she could. Eliot Hopkins was no writer. He was an inheritor, and he took that responsibility seriously.

"I've passed old Ray here a few times on my way up the hill and got curious about all the paraphernalia." Three weathered American flags were stuck into the ground at the base of the stone. Five baseballs, three caps, two fielder's gloves, and two rotten wooden bats (one with black electrical tape wound about the handle) rested against it. A plastic beer cup lay a small distance away next to a crumpled Cleveland Indians windbreaker. The final two items seemed to Eliot like garbage that the groundskeeper hadn't thrown away on account of the trash having landed close enough to Chapman's grave to be considered part of the memorial. A miniature, navy blue batting helmet had been placed in the center of the material encomium, the kind one might get in exchange for a quarter plunked into the gumball machine at any Cleveland-area grocery store. *Ironic*, Eliot thought.

"I wonder who left all this stuff. I mean, are there really Ray Chapman fans that make this a destination?"

"I guess," Eliot said. He pointed up the slight incline with his nose, not wanting to remove his hands from his coat pockets, or to disturb Alice's embrace. "Just a few more rows." They lingered for a long minute. Once they finally moved, Eliot scrutinized the plastic cup as they walked by it. The ink was mostly sun faded, but he could just make out Major League Baseball's official 1997 World Series logo set against a pale-yellow background. Next to it stood the dim red and blue silhouette of a pitcher in his follow-through. In a few more years, he thought, the cup would be entirely bleached by the elements, and no longer mistakable for an anachronistic tribute to Chapman, but the weathered trash it had become.

Olivia Hopkins's grave was bare. No one had deposited trinkets, ironic or otherwise, to commemorate her life. And Frank wouldn't bring out the artificial holiday wreath until after Thanksgiving. The headstone was rare, though not unique, in that it bore two birthdays: Olivia's and Eliot's. He pointed this out to Alice, who, again, had no words. The stone labeled Olivia as *Mother, Wife, & Daughter* as if she had been that thing first rather than last. Eliot always wondered at the inscription, maintaining that she never actually got the chance to be a mother. He had mentioned it to his father once, who looked right through him and said, "Yes. For nine months."

"So," Eliot said.

"I'm sorry," Alice said.

"Don't be. At least not about this. It'd be worse if I could remember her," he lied. "Like if I had been eight and all of a sudden she was gone. That would be harder." Eliot knew that Alice wanted to understand how he felt, and surprisingly, he wanted to help her, if only partially. "That's how old I was when my dad lost his legs. I can remember playing catch with him in the driveway of the Fire Station, and following him on my mountain bike through the trails at Euclid Creek Park. I think he had just taken my training wheels off the week before it happened."

"What happened? I mean, did it happen in a fire?" Alice asked.

"Cornell hit him with a car," Eliot said.

"Damn."

"Yeah. Believe it or not, they actually became friends *afterwards*."

"Really?"

"You know who Robert Prudent is?"

"No."

"Well, they did. Maybe the only two Samuel Beckett fans in Cleveland who were also into true crime. So Cornell, the story goes, visited my dad in the hospital the night of the accident dressed like a pimp for Halloween, and my dad, hopped up on pain killers, kept calling him Prudent."

"Okay, but who is Prudent?"

Eliot laughed. "Right, he's the pimp that stabbed Beckett in Paris, and then had the audacity to visit him at the hospital afterwards to ask for forgiveness."

"Weird."

"No doubt," Eliot said. "But they've been buds ever since."

Alice shook her head in near disbelief, "That's incredible. Your dad is pretty fantastic."

Eliot, staring down at his mother's name carved into a twenty-two year old granite slab, said, "I know." He tugged at Alice's arm, leading her back down the hill in the direction from which they had come, their feet sinking softly into the frozen grass. "My great-grandparents are over there." He pointed in the direction Alice thought to be north, toward the lake. Eliot was right, she couldn't see it, but she could imagine what it should look like from The Heights that afternoon: a Wedgewood blue basin capped by violent, white breakers, indistinguishable from the low-hanging Canadian clouds on the horizon. All around her walls of evergreen and Berea

Sandstone framed her imagined vision of the great lake churning like an overworked slushy machine. It was the same lake she had grown up with in Buffalo, and she recalled looking westward over the long expanse of water toward Detroit, whose polluted skies lit the setting sun a resplendent array of purples and pinks and oranges that seemed to erupt when it finally touched down against the horizon. She was cold, and the image of the nearly-frozen lake made her skin bristle. Still, she thought, there was something life affirming about the Erie frost. It was a test of one's existential fortitude. It had born presidents and millionaires, forged mythic lawmen and baseball gods, and encouraged the true romance of Eliot Hopkins and Alice Browne.

Eliot puzzled at what she might be thinking about, but couldn't guess. His own mind swirled like the chaotic waters enchanting Alice's imagination. He held her close to at least remind her of his presence if not the significance of the day. "You hungry?" he asked.

Her consciousness returned from across the waters. "Getting there," she said. They approached her car, which had begun to blend in with the increasingly overcast sky. "You should drive. I don't know how to get to the West Side Market." Alice tossed Eliot her keys. They caromed off his palm, which was too numb to catch them, but not numb enough to dull the sting of the cold metal against his skin. He retrieved the keys from a small pocket of frozen earth the shape of a grounds keeper's boot.

"Sure you'll be all right?" He asked. Alice suffered from motion sickness if she wasn't behind the wheel.

She had already peeled away from him toward the passenger-side door, "I'll be fine." She heard the lock click open as Eliot pushed the release button on her key. The door's rubber liner had begun to freeze to the frame, forcing Alice to tug at the handle coercively. They got into the car next to one another. Eliot turned the key in the ignition. A plume of white exhaust rolled from the muffler up the hatchback window. Alice pitched her purse into the back seat and dialed the heater further into the red. The vents blew brisk like an Alberta Clipper, startling both of them. She turned the fan to low while the car warmed. Eliot pressed each of the seat-warmer buttons and toyed with the navy-blue Cleveland Indians wristband that Alice kept slung around the gear shifter, which waited in the Purgatory of neutral for the cold-engine light to go out. Alice leaned over and kissed Eliot on the cheek.

"What was that for?" He asked, happily.

"Just, thank you," she said. "I know coming here probably wasn't high on your list this afternoon, but it was nice to see a new place."

"Yeah."

"And I learned about Ray Chapman!"

"That is true."

"And Cornell, and your dad," she said. "And you."

"You keep delving deeper into my backstory, which I didn't even know was all that interesting until we started dating," Eliot said. "Are you just using me for your novel?"

She slapped his arm, "Of course not! The story is basically done anyways. I've already sent out sample chapters to a few M.F.A. programs. You're just very interesting is all. In a good way."

Eliot returned her kiss, "Well, you're very easy to look at. In a good way."

"That doesn't make any sense," she said.

He knew that she was right. Even flirting should retain some sort of logic. He readied himself to try again. The cold engine light turned off and the air from the vents blew hotter, warming their hands and faces. Their seats had come alive, making it feel momentarily as if they had each peed in their pants. A yellow coupe sped past them.

"You're gorgeous is all, truly a manifestation of the beautiful person I've come to know over the past few weeks. It feels like we've been together forever; I can't believe I got the opportunity to know you at all." Eliot had felt like a total goof saying it, and Alice was more than slightly embarrassed to receive the compliment. It was probably the context, he reasoned. Better to have said it at lunch, holding hands across a café table, or walking arm-in-arm down one of the Market's produce aisles. But, it was true nonetheless. True enough to be said inside an idling automobile in the frozen cemetery where his unknown mother is buried. True enough, also, to warrant the response that Alice offered next.

Eliot reached down to release the parking break, but she stopped him. With her now functioning fingers, she unbuttoned her coat and worked her belt loose. She turned her hips toward him as he struggled to open her pants. The zipper gave way. He slid her jeans to her knees, revealing black lace and pink skin. Both of their hearts raced. She kissed his cheek again with her glossed mulberry lips, and her eyes hurriedly scanned the bitter landscape as he laid his head down in her lap. It had started to snow.

Alice rested her head against the seat back. Her eyes were open, and she watched as snowflakes melted, one-by-one, upon the windshield. In the brief instant before licking the warm glass Alice could make out each flake's unique, star-shaped fractal. The melting snowflakes vanished into droplets of water that coursed down the slant of tempered German glass in a slow, satisfying rhythm.

Alice stroked Eliot's hair, and her thoughts traveled to the way she had once lovingly held the thrashing head of a dying fawn. She had spotted it first. They were walking to Phoenix Coffee a few weeks earlier, the day Eliot had introduced her to Frank. The wounded fawn came into focus as they approached three Cleveland Heights bicycle cops on the east corner of

Coventry and Hampshire. They leaned against their bikes, looking silently at one another and at passing cars, refusing to acknowledge the wounded animal. She rushed forward as soon as she saw that the deer had not yet died, though it was clearly in its throes. The cops demanded that she stay clear, but she ignored them. The fawn's legs flailed and its head smacked audibly against the concrete sidewalk. She remembered Eliot saying that it must have wandered out of the cemetery, and one of the cops confirmed that it had been struck by a car on Mayfield road. He pointed toward the scene of the accident, before hauling itself to the safety of the sidewalk. They, the cops, were waiting for the Cuyahoga County Road Commission to arrive and "put it out of its misery." Alice had already begun that process: she sat cradling its head in her lap and stroking its neck. The fawn had stopped convulsing, though it continued to breath heavy.

Eliot looked up from her lap and seemed to Alice as helpless as the dying fawn before its eyes emptied of fear and gently closed. Her body shook as she recalled its final, seemingly thankful breath. Alice held the fawn for a few minutes after its passing. The police had seemed ashamed in the face of her compassion. To Eliot, it was the most generous act he would ever witness.

* * *

By the time they arrived at the West Side Market the gray slush in the parking lot had become substantial. Though they stepped carefully, Eliot could not prevent the cold muck from flowing over the tops of his sneakers. His feet were soaked. The sluice, however, appeared less problematic to Alice, who, Eliot assumed, had simply not been a resident of Northeast Ohio long enough, nor with enough continuity, to adjust from the slightly harsher Buffalo standard. Plus, she was wearing boots. *Winter in Buffalo.* The thought gave him a slight shiver. *How long does it take someone to become a Clevelander?* He wondered. *How long would it take him to become something other than a Clevelander?* For the first time he seriously considered what it might mean to leave Ohio, the bookshop, his dad. He and Alice had only addressed the possibility in passing: if Alice was accepted to the fine arts program in creative writing at New York University, he might have to root for the Yankees, they joked. He shook his head. *The Mets made better sense. A National League team, he could still pull for his Tribe and cultivate some impression of belonging in The Big Apple. Would he call it The Big Apple? Does anyone? Either way, the Mets were similarly terrible, so at least he would be prepared to deal with a double dose of disappointment come October.*

"What's up?" Alice asked.

"What do you mean?" Eliot said.

"Nothing, you were just shaking your head. I wondered what you were thinking about." They walked past the Great Lakes Brewing Company and slowed to enjoy the smells of fermenting beer before coming to a stop at the periphery of Market Square Park, waiting for the walk signal to usher them across the intersection.

"Oh. I got some snow in my shoe. It's okay." Eliot said. The lights changed, and cars slowed carefully to full stops on top of the packed snow. Alice and Eliot ventured out into West 25th Street, approaching the Market's main façade. "I can't believe you haven't been here yet," Eliot continued, "It might not look like much outside, but it's actually quite spectacular in the main hall. And, you know what, I think they actually sell Gypsy Coffee at the Market Café. We should pick up a bag after lunch."

"That's the coffee we had at the station? Our first night? That was good stuff!" Alice agreed. A woman with two, full brown paper grocery bags cradled in her arms held the door for them with her foot. "Thank you," Alice said, rushing forward to release the woman from her courtesy.

They walked through the main Market doors that swung wide below an expanse of high windows. The iconic clock tower, anchored to the southeast corner of the building, stood to their right, tenacious as cemetery evergreens against the blustering lake-effect snow. The door shut behind them. A disembodied pig's head grinned at the couple from a butcher's stall. Skinned ducks hung from hooks like halos above the swine's beaming face. Eliot raised a hand to shelter his nose from the offending stench, and squeezed a wordless apology through Alice's overcoat. He ushered her toward the produce annex and Maha's Falafel, chiding himself for taking her through the Main Hall, though he had wanted her to see the domed brick ceiling, and to experience the general bustle of Cleveland's gustatory epicenter.

"Sorry about that. I don't ever remember the smell being that offensive," he said once they had entered the small Egyptian eatery and landed at the end of a short line. He quickly counted five customers between them and falafel sandwiches.

"From one cemetery to another, right?" She said. Her analogy stunned him. Eliot hadn't thought of it that way, but certainly she was right. *Is this how artists perceive the world, like theoretical physicists charting the interconnectedness of all things via string theory? And even if experimental physicists couldn't prove string theory, the fact that artists could see all the pieces of the universe in this way, as somehow coherently linked, meant, in a very real way, that maybe no one could ever be fundamentally alone.* He studied Alice, who turned her attention to the shaky handwriting scrawled upon a large chalkboard swinging above the counter from what appeared to be fishing line. The sign swayed slightly. Its movement, coupled with the poor lettering gave her a small fit of motion sickness. She loosened her scarf, allowing the faint scent of her sugarplum perfume to escape from its tight swaddle. He envied her, and wondered if that was the same as love.

Eliot listened as the pair of women in front of Alice discussed the perils of love for an ill-fated couple in Nigeria. The way they spoke suggested to Eliot that Ifemelu and Obinze were characters in a book they had both recently read, or were currently reading, rather than actual acquaintances. He spied a bulky brown hardcover tucked into the armpit of the woman closest to Alice that seemed to match the book her friend clutched in her left hand, confirming, he thought, his suspicion concerning Ifemelu and Obinze. Curious, Eliot slung both arms around Alice and rested his chin on her left shoulder. He breathed in sugarplum and maneuvered to read the book's cover. He could only make out the word: 'Ngozi.' Eliot made a note to solve that puzzle later, figuring these few letters had disclosed enough information for Google, or Cornell, to fill in the blanks. Eliot had been actively searching for a book that could persuade him to cry, but hadn't been successful for a number of years. It wasn't exactly the kind of reading recommendation you could ask for, either. Too much depends not only on the story, but also the reader's disposition, even the environment in which the book is read.

The women in front of them had ordered spicy falafel sandwiches with white sauce and a pair of Fattoush Salads. Alice moved to the front of the line and greeted the man working the register. Eliot tried again to get a look at the book's cover but failed at adding any new information. Alice ordered, and the cashier said to Eliot, "Anything for you, sir?" Eliot turned his head to address the man behind the counter, who, he discovered, looked eerily like Joseph Kowalski Senior. *A universe of tangled strings.*

"I, uh, I'll have the same, please," Eliot said, recovering his composure. "Oh! And a red bean sesame ball."

"That sounds good," Alice said to Eliot. Then, to the man behind the counter, "Make it two!"

The old man, shoulders stooped low, read their order back to them confirming that he had everything correct. Alice exchanged cash for a laminated card with the number 74 printed on it in permanent black marker. "Set that on your table, please, and we'll bring everything out to you. Should be about five minutes." The man behind the counter also handed each of them a cloudy plastic cup filled with tap water and a thin slice of lemon that rested atop a few floating ice cubes.

"Thanks," Eliot said, already hurrying toward one of the only two empty tables remaining in the cramped café. The swell and ebb of the line crowded the table nearest the register, so he and Alice claimed the other table situated at the exact center of the room. Next to them, an elderly couple sat side-by-side rather than across from one another. Their feet touched beneath the table as their hands worked knives and forks with diminished precision. They were dressed handsomely. Overly dressed for lunch at a glorified food cart, Eliot and Alice agreed.

"So do you think there's something special about the place, or the date?" Alice asked Eliot, referring to their formal dress. "I wonder if we share an anniversary?" She joked. Their hats and scarves and gloves and overcoats were flawlessly coordinated, and the shine of their shoes, she pointed out, suggested they had somehow floated to their seats above the brine of the Cleveland streets.

"Maybe neither," Eliot said. The couple had each eaten half of their respective sandwiches, traded plates, and picked up where the other had left off. One nodded as if his taste buds were grooving to a jazz ensemble, the other fanned his fingers into a sign that would have signaled to any other Hepcats in the vicinity something like 'hot socks' or 'cat's pajamas.' He then dabbed a drop of tahini sauce from the corner of his mouth with a flimsy diner napkin.

Eliot took a minute to study the couple, and then continued, "They're from a greater generation. They probably wake up every morning and put on suits because that's just what you do when you get out of bed. They believe in something akin to magic because it had to be a force greater than luck that guided their families from the Old World safely across the Atlantic, and which delivered them into the arms of lovers who miraculously spoke a familiar language in a strange land, and then protected that love for nearly a century from foreign wars and medical complications and hydroplaning automobiles."

"Are you saying things were better then?" Alice asked.

"I'm saying it doesn't always seem like the same amount of enchantment exists in the world anymore."

"You put a spell on me," she offered.

"Well then," said Eliot, who had elected to sit across from Alice at the small, round aluminum table, "Maybe that *will* be us one day."

"We can hope so," she said.

"Yeah?" He asked her.

"Yeah," she said.

Eliot leaned back in his seat, and threw his right ankle across his left knee, taking up more than his fair share of space between the tables. He spied what he figured must be their order being carried toward the number 74 placard that Alice had shoved into the tall holder at the edge of the table. The women who were in front of them in line had already received their food and set their matching books aside to eat. Eliot quickly drained the remaining water from his cup, leaving the few ice cubes and lemon slice settled against the bottom in hopes that the server would offer him a refill. As the server approached, he saw the ticket number, 10, riding on the tray that was carried past the table.

"Sweet potato fries on top of the falafel?" Alice said, also watching the food pass them by. "I'll have to try that next time!"

"That's definitely an unexpected combination," he said, only half attentive.

"Genius."

"Listen—" Eliot began.

"I am," Alice filled the silence.

"Let's move in together."

"Wow, you went with the rip-off the band aid method, huh?"

"Not exactly." Eliot said, but was cut short by the arrival of their food. A different server, a younger version of the man behind the counter who had taken their order, asked if Eliot would like his water refilled. "Yes, please," he said, watching Alice muddle over what more he might have to say to her. The gentlemen to their right had stood up and were helping one another with their overcoats. They wrapped themselves in their scarves and collected their hats and gloves from the table before disappearing, arm-in-arm, into the Market.

"That's quite a proposal for a one-month anniversary," Alice said. "I'm obviously not opposed to the idea. I mean, I figured that was the plan for when we moved to NYU."

Eliot took a bite of his falafel, and recalled their recent trip to New York City. He set his sandwich down on the teal Fiestaware plate before him, wiped his lips of the stinging hot sauce, and pushed the tips of his fingers into his closed eyes. He used the gesture to buy a few seconds to think. The pressure felt good. "I bought a house." Eliot lowered his hands and opened his eyes.

Alice looked as he expected: surprised. "Really?" She asked. The restaurant was beginning to thin out. Except for the two women who had turned their attention from lunch to their books now spread before them, the lunch crowd had come and gone back to their offices. It was quiet, and they both instinctively spoke in hushed tones. "Where is it?"

"Cleveland. East 74th Street." Realizing that the street number would mean nothing to Alice other than it was on the opposite side of the Cuyahoga River from their present locale, he added, "It's not even a nice part of town." And then, "I'm sorry."

The server hadn't returned to re-fill his water glass and Eliot's mouth had gone dry. He tried to clear his throat of the phlegm that had built up as he became increasingly nervous. *Ackem! Hermch!* It was a trait that both his mother and father had passed on to him. He wondered if it was a Slovenian thing.

She was confused. "Then why did you buy it? And why would you want us to live there?" Alice wasn't really looking for an answer to either of those questions, but didn't know how to get to her primary concern, which was the fact that Eliot seemingly did not want to move to New York City with her, and further, wanted her to abandon her plans of attending NYU in the fall.

"I got detoured," he said.

Alice considered his explanation, albeit vague, as good as any she might have expected. "Okay. So what does that mean?"

"I mean literally detoured. I was heading back from a job, the lighting gig at John Carroll, the day I met you, the day before the night I met you in the station. It was raining—"

"I remember, I had class that morning and got soaked walking back to Campion," Alice said, not knowing that Eliot had seen her.

"We were digging trenches for the underground wiring, but the storm made it impossible, so we called it a day. I had a company truck that I had to take back to the shop downtown, and Cedar was closed for some utility work. The gas station attendant told me to take 74th Street to Central Ave., so I did. And when I got to the corner, I just saw this house that I sort of recognized from somewhere. It was pretty surreal. I sat there, trying to remember something I had never seen before. Then, finally I figured it out. I *had* seen it, or I'd seen a photograph of it at least."

"What? Like a for-sale listing?" Alice asked.

"No, an actual photograph. One I'd found mixed in with old pictures of my mom. It was in a box my dad keeps."

"Interesting."

"Yeah, well, there was this large bay window out front. I just wanted to take a peek inside, see what it looked like. I guess I was trying to imagine how they might have lived in that house. When I got to the door, Joe answered."

"Who?" Alice asked.

"Remember the old man I told you about when we passed through Poughkeepsie on the train from Albany?"

"The history teacher? It was his house?"

"Yes. But even before it was his house, it had belonged to my great-grandparents."

Alice brightened. Her brow furrowed into a series of creases that Eliot had begun to refer to as 'thinkles.' Their appearance at this time confused him—a lot. He certainly hadn't expected the home's provenience to be its selling point, yet somehow Alice's demeanor had softened—a little.

"I'm not sure how long Joe had been watching me, waiting for me to get curious enough to leave the truck. He invited me in, and for some reason I couldn't turn him down, so we got to talking about the house and baseball and Cleveland more generally. Then I saw this list of names carved into a door frame. The names belonged to my great-grandparents and their kids, including my grandma."

"Your mom's mother?"

"Yeah. She was born in the house just before they moved to Neff Road."

Alice shook her head in disbelief: "What?! That's crazy!"

"In retrospect, it's some coincidence that I ended up there…and on the day we met."

"Like some sort of cosmic plan."

"I wouldn't go that far."

"Wouldn't you?" She was disappointed. If she was going to abandon her plans, then she wanted to believe that the universe had a plan of its own. And she certainly wanted Eliot to believe with her. "How much?" She asked.

"Thirty thousand."

"Wow! You can barely buy a car for thirty thousand dollars. So, how bad is the neighborhood? Or, is the place just unlivable?"

"It's actually a pretty nice house. The outside needs a facelift—new windows, a coat of paint, maybe a new fence—but the inside was well taken care of. And the problem with the neighborhood isn't so much that it's dangerous. It's just more-or-less sad." Eliot oversold the area in hopes of further softening Alice to the idea of building a life with him behind those four walls.

"By my estimation that describes about ninety percent of Cleveland," she said, not at all joking.

"Okay… it's really sad," Eliot said, less-than-half-heartedly, affirming her judgment of his city.

"That's why I thought we were getting out of here. Moving to Manhattan!" She tried to muster up some excitement for the prospect by taking hold of his hand and widening her eyes to the point that he couldn't look anywhere but at his own reflection staring back from the black pools of her pupils. He was terribly in love.

"I know," he conceded, "but this doesn't necessarily stop us from relocating if we don't want to stay. Look, I've been working two jobs since I was sixteen, so I just paid for it in full. It was only about half my savings. So, I've got another thirty thousand that we can put into the house.

"I don't want to stay, Eliot." Alice cut him off.

A long moment of silence settled between them.

"Well," Eliot recovered, "then I've got some money that we can rely on in addition to your stipend. I guess I could sell it, or maybe rent it," he said as the thought entered his mind. "Maybe Cornell would be interested. He's always talking about moving closer to the shop. If it's too cold to ride his motorcycle, he spends half his day waiting for buses."

Alice sighed, and after another uncomfortably long pause, the kind that always seems to precede a responsible turn in the conversation, asked, "What about your dad?" She figured that Eliot's hesitance to leave Cleveland had little to do with himself, and even less to do with Cornell. She had been wondering ever since returning from their East Coast trip why anyone would elect to live in the rusted out cities and sprawling suburbs that creep along the winding coastline of America's Great Lakes: Milwaukee, Detroit, Cleveland, Buffalo—she could admit that her hometown was not exempt from the list, but wasn't sure that Eliot could be as honest. He was, after all, an Indians fan. She meant that as a compliment. He was the sort of person who, like most Clevelanders she had met, could love almost unconditionally, year after dreadful year, as they both sunk further into the mire of life. He was a man so foolishly optimistic about the future and yet so cynical in the present that he could only cling to the immortal promise of 'next year.'

"Yeah. I don't know," Eliot said about the fate of his father. "He'd be fine, I think. If I left, I mean. It's not like we wouldn't ever visit, or that he'd never come out to New York. Plus, who knows where we'd end up when you finished school, anyway."

Alice was heartened by his response. "The problem is that writers can't make it on their work alone. I mean, I'm not drafting scripts for Hollywood. I'll need a teaching job, and the likelihood of landing one that allows me enough time to work on my own projects depends a lot on where I get my degrees," Alice explained to Eliot the importance of academic pedigree. "Plus," she added, "the chances of getting hired at a school in Cleveland are basically nonexistent. Who knows where we'll end up when I'm finished school."

"I know," he conceded.

"Eliot."

"Yeah?"

Alice hesitated. She knew this was the end, though she wasn't certain who was abandoning whom. She almost smiled: *the true definition of tragedy.* "I got in."

"To NYU?" Eliot asked.

"Everywhere. My early decision letters came yesterday," she admitted.

"That's great! But why didn't you tell me?" Eliot figured that he hadn't been doing as good of a job hiding his actual feelings about the possible move as he thought he was doing. He was some mixture of embarrassed and ashamed that calculated into an acute sense of remorse. *I'm ruining her life*, he thought.

They were now the only two remaining in the small café situated off the main hall of the West Side Market. Their falafel sandwiches remained half eaten and Eliot's water glass had not been refilled. His left leg bounced nervously beneath the table where Alice couldn't see it, though she felt a slight shake through the floor and knew from it that he hadn't been expecting this news for another couple of weeks. She placed her hand on his knee, bringing it to an abrupt halt. "I was waiting for the right time. Today. I wanted to give you New York as an anniversary present."

"Oh," Eliot said. He was as surprised as he was impressed. Over the course of their month-long relationship he had been reading her work: a smattering of old short stories she had printed out and given to him at regular intervals of about two per week. He still had not read a single word of her novel, but Alice's stuff was good, and he didn't doubt that she would get into at least a couple of programs. But he hadn't prepared himself for what that would actually mean for their relationship. That she had gotten into all of the top writing programs on the merits of her undergraduate thesis was simply astounding. He was unfailingly proud of her, and now mightily curious about her novel. Eliot knew, in that moment of pride and wonder, that there was no place for him in her life. He could not leave Cleveland, but he also couldn't tell Alice—not now. He was scared, and could think of nothing better to say than "Thanks."

"You don't seem very enthused."

"No. I am. I just like it here. You know? I like that you've got to have a strong heart to make it in a town that's cold and gray for six months out of the year. I like that we're willing to suffer for our loves, year-in and year-out. This place demands an enduring spirit."

"You're saying Sinatra had it all wrong?"

"Huh?

"*New York, New York.* You know, 'If I can make it there, I can make it anywhere.'"

"Oh, yeah, I don't know. All I'm saying is that Cleveland deserves people like you." It was the greatest compliment he could think to give her.

"I love you, you know," Alice said.

"Thanks." He knew she was gone, even if she hadn't yet realized it. "I love you, too."

"I'm really very happy we found each other," She said.

"Me too." The server returned to their table with a fresh glass of water. Eliot thanked him, exchanging his empty glass for the full one and drank deeply.

"How's the Lake Erie High Ball?" Alice asked.

Eliot lowered his eyes. He was going to miss the way Alice could describe a glass of water.

* * *

They arrived at the house about an hour later. Alice pulled into the cracked driveway that ran along the south side of the property. She stopped flush with the porch, and yanked hard on the emergency brake, placing her car into park. When they got out of the car she noticed that the street was empty. She felt exiled from the rush of humanity they both experienced at the West Side Market. Eliot watched as Alice eyed the liquor store across the street, and then the Laundromat opposite it on the other side of Central Avenue. Finally, she scanned the boarded windows and barred doors that shackled each of the other houses as far as she could see from her spot in the driveway. The landscape did not summon visions of idyllic summers spent writing on the porch, or hanging laundry from a clothesline strung between two apple trees—two things she might have done regularly after graduation had she not been planning to leave. There was something peaceful, she thought, about watching clothes dry while filling blank, white pages with lines of dense, black ink.

"So this is it?" She asked.

"This is it," he confessed.

"And you want to live here? You want *us* to live here?"

Eliot shoved his hands into the deep wells of his pockets, fishing his fingers around for something, anything, but catching nothing. He wondered where he had placed his tube of lip balm, which typically rested against his thigh in his left pant pocket. Suddenly his lips felt unendurably dry and he licked at them to ease their irritating chap. The wind had picked up, and snowflakes blew sideways into their eyes without respite. "Let's go inside."

Alice allowed him to usher her through the gate, still askew on its screaming hinges, and up the brief stone walk to the uncertain steps that would take them inside the enclosed porch and out of the wind if not the cold. Eliot entered first. Alice followed, eagerly looking over his right shoulder at a pile of boxes sitting atop an elevated wooden platform about ten feet long by four feet wide. Her first thought was that Eliot had already begun to move his things from his dad's apartment on Coventry Road. A few of the boxes, however, were opened and she could see a roll of white cotton in one and what looked to be a small light wheel—orange and green and blue and red—poking out from another. The two items didn't compute. "What's all this?" she asked curiously. The not-so-subtle hint of frustration that had accompanied her earlier questions had transformed into genuine interest.

"This," Eliot said triumphantly, extending his arms in either direction toward the two poles of the plywood, "is a Christmas platform! My grandpa made it."

"What do you mean 'made it'?"

"He and his Dad, my great-grandpa, the one who lived in this house, they built it." Eliot opened a third box and removed a large wooden farmhouse and held it before her. "There are, I think, seven buildings in all: two farms, a blacksmith's shop, three houses, a church…and the manger. So eight."

"They look like little log cabins," she said. Eliot handed the farm to Alice for her to inspect. She ran her fingers along the long cherry twigs covered in a smooth, brownish lacquer.

"I guess so," Eliot said. "My grandpa told me once that he and his dad had collected the twigs from a grove of cherry trees behind Borromeo Seminary when he was just a little boy, maybe ten or eleven years old."

"In Wickliffe, right?"

"Yeah, next to All Saints. And the stones that they used for the chimneys were collected from the Euclid Creek Reservation." Eliot handed her one of the houses in exchange for the barn. Alice ran her fingers across the smooth stones. They were various shades of pink and green and gray. At the top of the chimney, she spotted a small round hole that was lined with a badly oxidized copper band. She scraped at the surface of it with her pinky, which was slightly too big to fit through the circle. "The chimneys actually work," Eliot explained, "It's hooked up to some sort of small humidifier."

"This is marvelous."

"Just wait until you see the whole thing set up and in motion. They crafted trees and figurines of farm hands, mail carriers, lantern lighters, carolers, carriage drivers, ice skaters, and a whole nativity scene. Plus, there's a train that runs around the whole thing." Eliot had seen it so many times that he could envision it even before the cotton snow was laid out across the plywood base. He thought of his grandpa, likely the same way the old man remembered his own father whenever the little town came to life: a magic trick he never really understood until now. "I used to set this up with my Grandpa every year, the day after Thanksgiving," he said. "They had a porch kind of like this one."

"You told me your holiday tradition was watching movies with your dad," Alice said.

"I guess I have a couple of traditions."

"So, why is it here? I mean, why isn't it still at your grandpa's house?"

"He actually passed away last year," Eliot said. "On Christmas."

"Oh." She fit her arm around Eliot's waist and kissed his neck. "Let's set it up."

"It's a bit early," he said.

"So what? You're planning to put it up anyway, right?"

"Of course."

"You don't want to do it alone, do you? And I'll be in Buffalo for Thanksgiving. So let's put it up now." Alice had already removed a long section of split-rail fence from the box containing the light wheel and was unraveling it along the border of the platform. Eliot watched her, wondering if she was beginning another tradition of her own.

"Okay. But we have to put the snow down first," he instructed, removing the cotton from the box and motioning for Alice to take down the fence she had just finished installing. She looked back at him over her shoulder, smiling like he had never seen her smile before. Her hair was a mess from having recently pulled off her knit hat, and her cheeks were still flushed from the few moments they had been exposed to the wind as they surveyed the neighborhood from the drive. Last winter he had lost his Grandpa to pneumonia, and this year he would move out of his father's house. For the moment, Alice filled the void left by the very different absences of both men.

The pair set to work under the direction of Eliot, who reluctantly took over as platform foreman. They began by unrolling the old cotton blanket that would serve as a layer of snow beneath the village bridges and skating rinks and houses. They set the barn at the far left of the scene, allowing ample space for the free-range ceramic animals. At the center, they set up the manger, which looked out of place to both of them in this cozy European Christmas village, but neither said anything about it. Train tracks bisected the platform, dividing country from the town where the houses, church, and townsfolk were set up. They laid flat strips of intersecting cobblestone streets upon the cotton, and placed carriages hauling evergreen trees facing toward the town square. Alice arranged a miniature sleigh and its eight reindeer atop one of the homes as Eliot, having finished laying the railroad track, set the American Flyer in motion with the flick of a switch.

The entire village came to life: lights shone from the stained glass windows lining either side of the church, a red glow escaped from the blacksmith's shop, lead figurines skated on the pond, pulled along by magnetic strips while executing Biellmann spins and Bauer glides. Gas lamps flared, vaporized water smoked white from the chimneys, and a music box at the base of the ski slopes played Louis Armstrong's rendition of "White Christmas."

"It's magical," Alice said.

"It kind of is," Eliot agreed.

They stood together on the porch of Eliot's tall house looking at the splendor of what they had assembled and listening to an old man dream about the merrier Christmases of yesteryear. It was dark outside. The streetlights had failed to turn on, and no light escaped from the other buildings surrounding the house at the corner of East 74th Street and Central Avenue. Not even the occasional beam of a car's headlamp pierced the dread of that frozen intersection. Had anyone ventured down the broken road, they would have seen two kids imbuing it with new life, illuminated by the steady, slow oscillations of fifty-year-old color wheel.

"Shall I make us some coffee?" Eliot asked.

"Yes, please. My fingers have gone numb. Geeze, how long have we been out here?"

"Probably a couple hours. I can't believe you haven't been inside yet."

"I am a bit curious," Alice admitted.

Eliot opened the heavy wooden door, and invited her into the foyer, "After you." He clasped her hand as she walked by, arresting her in the doorway. They pulled close and offered one another a kiss. She looked back at the whimsy of their labor, he into the bosom of the house. Neither of them knew what the other was thinking, and if they were being completely honest with themselves, neither was entirely certain of the thoughts parading through their own minds either.

Inside, the house looked like it belonged to a senior citizen—smelled like it, too. *Mothballs. Cliché*, Alice thought. An ivory-colored couch, covered in fitted plastic, sat beneath the large bay window that looked out onto the porch and the well-lighted Christmas Platform. A 26" cathode ray tube television sat atop a hand-carved stereo cabinet at the far end of the living room. To the left, an archway opened into the dining room where a piano sat flush against the wall shared with the kitchen.

"Where did you get all this stuff?" Alice asked.

"Joe left it. He said he didn't need it anymore, and that it might as well stay with the house. I could do with it what I please."

"So what are you going to do with it?"

"Well, I'll probably take the plastic off the couch, at least." They both snickered, remembering their grandparents' Davenports covered with a similar protective shield. "And the TV has to go. Otherwise, most of the stuff is in really nice condition."

It was already a home, Alice realized. She hadn't thought anything of it when Eliot offered to make her a cup of coffee, but seeing the furniture neatly arranged helped her understand that Eliot had been living there. Electricity powered the American Flyer and color wheel on the porch—that should have been her first clue. The radiated heat should have been her second. They had spent most of their time together touring Cleveland and hanging out behind the bookstore. And when they did hunker down for a quiet evening Eliot would crash in her dorm room. Somewhere in between their shared experiences, while she was attending class and writing her book, Eliot had moved his life here.

He disappeared around the corner into the kitchen, and Alice sat down on the piano bench. She began to hum even before her fingers landed on the worn keys, lightly drumming Chopin's Berceuse Op. 57 D Flat Major from memory. High ceilings provided the room with excellent acoustics, so that Alice could feel the notes vibrate against her body. Her back rounded as she sank further into the piano bench and the song. She hadn't played in months. All of her free time had been spent writing or hanging out with Eliot. She felt pleasantly alone with the instrument. Her eyes closed, and except for the controlled chaos of her fingers moving along the keyboard, it looked as if she had fallen asleep. She focused on the dim yellow glow of a nearby floor lamp that brightened the underside of her eyelids. Shapes floated across the black expanse, and she found that she could manipulate them by squeezing her eyes shut tighter, or relaxing them to the point of almost opening. The smell of ground coffee wafted in from the next room and mingled with the piano's lullaby. Her fingers came to a rest in the dimples that had been pressed into the ivory keys throughout years of use. She allowed them to wade there as she slowly opened her eyes, bringing Eliot into focus.

He leaned against the archway that led to the kitchen, his shoulder propping him up. He handed a mug of coffee to Alice, who wallowed in its warmth. Eliot cupped both hands around his own mug and lifted it to his lips. He sucked the liquid into his mouth with a loud slurp, something Alice still had not gotten used to even after he explained that the slurp helped to aerate the brew, unlocking the subtler flavors. She tried and conceded that he was right, but his rightness didn't make it seem any less silly.

"That was beautiful," Eliot said. "I didn't know you played."

"My parents forced me to take lessons starting in the second grade. I hated it. All the Stephen Foster campground songs, ughck! But, eventually, they let me choose my own songbooks so I stuck with it."

"You're really good."

"Not really good, but okay. And this piano is nicely tuned. It's no worse for the wear."

"It's yours," Eliot offered.

"Oh, I don't have anywhere to put it, and moving it—"

"Put it right there. Just leave it where it is." Then he added, "You know, it's worth more than the house."

Alice stood up from the bench as if retreating from the idea, and walked into the kitchen. The room looked exactly as it had when Eliot sat across from Joseph Kowalski Sr. only a month earlier. Its walls were painted tangerine orange and the cupboards were cream colored. She couldn't be certain if the painter had tried to make it look like a 1950s soda shop or an homage to the Cleveland Browns. Strangely, it worked. A green tea kettle sat atop an electric stove, wine bottles lined the shelves above the refrigerator. A set of vintage china and a bowl of fruit were stacked delicately on the counter. On the opposite wall stood a bookshelf overstuffed with coffee paraphernalia: two burr grinders (mechanical and hand-crank), a glass Chemex, two ceramic single-cup coffee drippers, a stainless steel French press, a hand kettle, an assortment of paper and metal filters, a scale, three bags of coffee, an unopened chicory tin from Café du Monde, and a dozen or so diner mugs from coffee houses across the United States.

Next to the bookcase—on the kitchen table along with Eliot's cell phone, wallet, and an old Remington 585-M pocket knife (a birthday present from his father)—rested the familiar copy of *Flannery O'Conner's Complete Stories*. Alice set down her coffee and picked up the book. She opened it to the story that she had marked earlier that week: "A Good Man is Hard to Find." It was one of her favorite stories and she meant to re-read it before leaving for Thanksgiving Break, but hadn't. She still remembered her introduction to it in Professor Hayes's class. He had read the opening pages aloud to them, or rather had attempted to do so. He made it as far as the second paragraph in which the narrator describes the children's mother as having a face as broad and innocent as a cabbage. He was overcome by a fit of glorious laughter. He couldn't stop. His students began laughing. They couldn't stop. It was the most perfect interaction she had had with literature inside of a college classroom. She remembered thinking, *I wish I could do that*. She laughed.

"What's so funny?" Eliot asked. He had spun in the doorway so that his left shoulder now propped his body up against the archway. Alice wiped happy tears from her eyes, causing Eliot to rub at his eye with the hand not holding his coffee mug; the curl of his index finger massaged beneath his glasses.

"Nothing. I was just remembering Bailey's wife and her cabbage face," she giggled.

Eliot's mouth twisted into a grin and he snorted through his nose. He finished rubbing his eye, increasingly worried about his inability to engage a text emotionally beyond a small grin or a dry frown, and entered the kitchen where he sat down on the bench that ran along the backside of the table. Alice slid in next to him and rested her head on his shoulder, which is when she noticed the list of names carved into the doorframe across the room: Ned, Mary, Ruth, Yuri, Muriel, Florence, Jacob, Charlie, Madeline, 1st Lt. LaRose, Mary, Emily, Abigail, Junior, Jane, Joseph, Eliot. "That's it?"

"A list of everyone who has lived in this house. Yuri through Madeline, that's my family."

Alice re-read the final name carved into the wood: Eliot. "I see you've made your choice."

Eliot brushed her hair behind her ear so that he could see the profile of her eye, which was staring straight across the room. "I'm sorry," is all he could muster.

They sat in silence, savoring their coffee one another's presence, each of them trying in their own way to record the memory of it all.

"It's okay," Alice assured him. Eliot knew she would be fine, but wasn't so sure about himself. Then Alice unexpectedly reached for the Remington blade lying closed on the table in front of her. It fit snugly in her palm, and she was able to twirl it about easily with her fingers. The blade was small, about three-and-a-half inches long, and it couldn't have weighed more than an ounce. She used her thumb to flick it open, then stood up from the table and moved away from Eliot with purpose toward the carved doorframe. Eliot remained silent as he watched her kneel down before the growing list and scratch her name deep into the old wood beneath his.

An Historiography of Love in Three Parts: III
April 18, 1922

YURI ZUPANČIČ walked through the kitchen wearing dark grey trousers and a white cotton undershirt. He wore suspenders and a navy blue Cleveland Indians baseball cap, which he had placed upon his head every morning since attending the 1921 American League Pennant Game with Muriel's Uncle Victor. He carried a crate holding twelve empty wine bottles the color of Calce olives. A large mahogany box coupled with a brass horn speaker sat atop the kitchen counter broadcasting the Cleveland Indians versus the St. Louis Browns baseball game. The device had cost Yuri just over a week's worth of salary, but promised him front row seats at every game—even when his team was on the road!

While the young couple moved their things from Bernadette and Victor's home a few blocks away, they listened as the Tribe socked the Browns 17-2. "That's a good start to the season! Five and Oh! Maybe we won't have to endure another New York Giants versus New York Yankees World Series this year," Yuri hoped.

Muriel had stopped listening when she noticed scratches in the doorjamb separating the kitchen from a small toilet room near the stairs leading into the cellar. "Yuri, look."

Yuri set down the box of wine bottles at the top of the stairs and joined his wife in the doorway.

"Ned and Mary carved their names into the jamb here." She ran her hand across the names. "And little Ruth, too." She placed her hand atop Yuri's, which he had set upon her shoulder. She looked up at him and asked, "Should we add ours as well?"

Yuri pulled the latest model Remington 585-M Jack Knife from his pocket (a housewarming gift from his pals at the office), and handed it to Muriel. She carefully opened the blade and set it against the wood to carve Yuri's name, then her own, and finally that of their daughter, Florence. All the while Yuri stood behind her with his hands rested on her shoulders, admiring her work and the gentle brush of her hair upon his fingers.

(Im)Permanence
November 13, 2013

"I'VE GOT AN APPOINTMENT with Igor," Eliot said.

"Which one?" asked the man behind the counter.

"There's more than one?"

The man offered only an annoyed smirk while Eliot stood before him, wondering what he had gotten himself into.

Alice had agreed to stay in Cleveland and build a life with him. Eliot decided to get a tattoo as a pledge of allegiance to Alice and her craft. Now he wasn't so sure that he hadn't made a painful mistake. The constant drone of three or four tattoo machines vibrating somewhere in the back of the shop sounded like thousands of snake scales rubbing against one another in an overpopulated viper pit. His skin bristled.

Eliot had met one of the two Igors over the summer at B Side on Coventry. Eliot was spending his Friday night plunking quarters into the Galaga machine trying to kill a few innocuous hours before he had to head over to the radio station for his weekly blues show. Igor was booked as the house DJ for the evening and had been spinning a lot of what he called nu-disco beneath European female pop vocalists, which Eliot kind of liked. They found occasion to talk due to the fact that they both happened to be wearing the same Cleveland Indians cap––navy blue with a white 'C' in the center. Eliot's was an original; Igor's a throwback.

When Igor was able to steal a couple of minutes away from his computer he asked Eliot what he thought of their chances. The Tribe had finished out July strong enough to revive the city's hopes for a playoff run even though that particular night they had lost 10-0 to Miami, which was doubly painful for those Cleveland faithful who still hadn't gotten over LeBron's decision to take his talents to South Beach. Eliot recalled saying something like sixty and forty-nine isn't a bad record heading into August. But, it isn't great either. Igor agreed. When they shook hands to part ways, Eliot noticed that Igor had the 1946 Chief Wahoo tattooed on his left hand, and asked him where he got it done, which was when Igor pulled a business card from his breast pocket and handed it to him before walking away.

"What's your name?" The guy-behind-the-counter asked with a phony smile that revealed a gold-capped tooth.

"Eliot."

"Sign these waivers, and I'll let him know you're here. Should be just a few minutes."

"Okay," Eliot said and signed on each of the blank lines. He felt lost in this foreign place, and so decided it best to do what he was told without question. It was a thoroughly Midwestern character flaw that he had been trying to amend since he became painfully aware of it in the tenth grade when he found himself at the sketchy end of Cain Park. He had been pulled there by the groove of about ten black street musicians playing Arthur Griswold's "Pretty Mama Blues" and sipping homebrew grain alcohol from mason jars. One of the men who he later came to know as Po' Sam handed him a bottle and told him to drink up. Eliot, the only white kid in sight, and not wanting to seem any further out-of-place, took a mouthful and promptly spat it to the ground. Tears welled in his eyes as the residual liquor burned ulcers into the soft tissue of his cheeks and tongue. His gums swelled and later bled. Po' Sam told the boy to "sip it shallow," and he did as he was told despite the pain.

Since his first encounter with Po' Sam, whenever Eliot Hopkins felt out of place, as if he had hopped aboard the wrong moving train under the blindness of night, he would place his unrestricted trust in complete strangers. In the case of the tattooed man with the pink beard and stretched ears, Eliot figured he was just doing his job. He sat the pen down across the paper he had carelessly signed and turned to hunker down in one of the red plastic chairs lining a wall decorated with tattoo designs: swallows, anchors, and roses monopolized the space. He slouched into the chair and waited.

Fifteen minutes later the counter attendant reappeared from the back and said, "It'll just be a few more minutes, he's setting up his station."

"Cool," Eliot said. The wait had only served to increase his doubts, and he began to think that maybe he should just abandon his deposit and leave the shop unscathed.

He resolved to do just that when Igor came out from the back to retrieve him: "Hey man, good to see you again. Too bad about that Wild Card game, huh?"

"What?" Eliot asked.

"The Tribe," Igor explained.

"Oh, yeah. Bummer."

"You ready?"

"I guess so," Eliot said. He again felt pulled toward a future that he couldn't recognize.

"Let me show you what I drew up, and then we can size it. You still thinking you want to do this on your shoulder?" Igor was the same height as Eliot, but about fifty pounds heavier. He wore his hair long and his clothes loose. He looked sloppy, but his artwork was clean.

"Yeah," Eliot said as the two entered a small, sectioned off space near the back of the parlor where Igor had covered his chair and stainless steel work table in cling wrap, and laid out six plastic thimbles that he would later fill with various inks.

An outlining needle and a set of shading needles lay on the table still wrapped in their sterile packaging next to his machine and a roll of paper towels.

Igor pulled a sheet of tracing paper from the top drawer of a Craftsman toolbox that he used as a filing cabinet and handed it to Eliot. "What do you think?" The whole design was about the size of a cabbage. At its center was a vintage diner mug with coffee flowing over the brim like *The Great Wave off Kanagawa*. Steam rose from the brew, spelling out *Alice* in ethereal lettering above the tsunami. On the front of the mug was a snowflake that, upon closer inspection, was composed entirely of the boulevards and avenues surrounding John Carroll University. At its center was the intersection of South Belvoir and Washington—the radio station where Eliot had met Alice Browne on a mysteriously snowy October evening. Framing the base of the mug sat an open book, its spine darkly shaded and its pages blank.

"It looks good," Eliot said. "Great…. It's exactly what I had imagined."

"Cool. What do you think about the size?"

"It's a little big, but I really like the detail, so I guess we shouldn't mess with it too much?"

"Yeah, it'll be hard to get all those streets done right if we shrink it."

"You're the boss," Eliot said and handed Igor the paper.

"Sounds good. Let me make a stencil and we can get to work." He left the room to run the image through a thermal copier, and when he came back told Eliot to take his shirt off and grab a seat. Igor pulled on a pair of latex gloves, and threaded the outlining needle into his machine while Eliot slung a leg over the high-backed chair to sit facing the opposite direction. Once the stencil was adhered, Igor filled two of the plastic thimbles with black ink.

"You ready?" he asked, revving the tattoo machine to prepare Eliot for the sting.

"Guess so," Eliot said, and set his jaw. The machine rattled a final warning before it bit, injecting its venom into the deep of his skin.

* * *

While Eliot made his love permanently visible, Alice Browne stood alone among a pile of cardboard boxes that contained what she thought were all of her worldly possessions, watching her mother drive away in a now empty U-Haul cargo van. She waved through the frosted front door, unsure if her mom could see her until she finally heard two short blasts of the horn before the van turned right onto Central Avenue toward East 55th and Interstate 90. She closed the door and slid the deadbolt into place. Alice Browne was home.

It was strange being there without Eliot. She hadn't considered that he might not be back from his mysterious 'appointment' when she arrived. And now, standing amid the boxes she and her mother had unloaded themselves, stopping only to hunt down a proper lunch, which included a ten-minute drive to Public Square and a couple of vegan burgers and a side of deep-fried pickles at a peculiar place called The Flaming Ice Cube, Alice doubted the rightness of her decision to move to Cleveland.

Nonetheless, she resolved to dig in and began distributing her belongings to their proper rooms, saving the actual unpacking for later. She effortlessly slid the boxes marked *kitchen* across the carpeted living-room floor, past the Ivers upright piano, and onto the linoleum tile. She then hoisted her toiletries, box-by-box, up the stairs and into the master bathroom before fetching the translucent, plastic containers stuffed with clothes that also had to be hauled up the stairs and into their bedroom. Those bulging eclectic boxes that she had labeled *stuff* Alice left in the living room where she imagined she and Eliot would eventually set up a more modern television across from the couch.

As promised, Eliot had removed the clear, plastic covering from the couch, and Alice crashed into the plush fabric, throwing her feet up onto one of the remaining boxes that she had pulled close enough to serve as an ottoman. There were no overhead lights, she noticed, but the floor lamps lit the room with a cozy, honey-colored glow that reminded her of the Four-Faced Liar so she didn't much mind. It felt homey, yet still unlike a home. She was certain that she would feel differently once Eliot was there and they had set up her workroom.

Alice walked up the long flight of stairs for the first time without a box cradled in her arms. There was a landing midway, which she figured had been useful to the home's previous owner. She paused briefly to look out a small window that faced the neighboring house only a few yards away. It had a matching window that was currently shuttered. No lights were on, which caused her to wonder just how alone she actually was on East 74th Street. At the top of the stairs, Alice took her time to look around. Of the two rooms she had not yet entered one was completely empty; a riotous mid-century wallpaper clung like new in the small room. It would have to go. The other was painted plain and furnished with an army-green loveseat and a dark coffee table littered with back issues of *History Magazine* and *Smithsonian*. A swiveling hardwood chair sat before a Dutch mahogany roll top desk, the sort that looked to her as if everything written upon it would be consequential. She thumbed through the drawers, unsure really of what she might even be looking for, but found that each of them had been emptied of past contents. Alice sat down in the chair and imagined writing her second novel in that very spot, listening to Velvet Underground albums and banging on the sturdy keys of an old typewriter.

She leaned back in her chair and envisaged the heat of a mid-August sun filtering in through the high windows, just like it had in an old photograph she had recently seen of Grand Central Station's main concourse. The rays would warm her face and her imagination. She hummed a few bars of "Pale Blue Eyes" before lifting herself out of the wooden chair, making a note to find a suitable cushion for extended writing sessions. Then, like a maiden cartographer filling in geographical voids, Alice voyaged out of the room that would be her own, and up another flight of stairs to the third floor—higher, even, than Eliot had yet ventured.

Joseph Kowalski Sr. had inexplicably left behind so much of his life that she couldn't help but wonder what sort of relics might have been abandoned in the attic. She wound her way up yet another curving staircase, her shoeless feet feeling the temperature drop with each upward step. When she finally pushed open the bi-fold door at the top of the stairs, she saw that it wasn't an attic at all, but a sort of archive—cold, musty. She entered the room to see what there was to be found.

Mostly it was neatly-arranged piles of obsolete encyclopedias and garbage bags filled with holiday decorations. An old vacuum cleaner stood in the corner next to a bowling ball bag and a couple of wooden tennis racquets. Two matching dressers had been pushed back-to-back with their drawers facing out. On top, Joe, she guessed, had unfurled a map of the Greater Cleveland Railway, Street Car, and Motor Coach Routes dated 1948. Each corner was held in place by a face-up silver dollar. A number of intersections had been circled in the black gloss of a grease pencil. Alice was unable to decipher any connection among them, though it did look as if one of the circles was drawn around East 74th Street and Central Avenue, of which she would have a bird's eye view if she were to look out the east-facing window at the front of the room.

She tugged at one of the wobbly knobs to open a dresser drawer, and found that it was filled with Motown 45s. She flipped through the top few, pausing long enough to read each artist's name: Letha Jones & The Rivals, Mabel John, Eugene Remus. She hadn't heard of any of them, and made a point to see if there was a record player tucked away among Joe's things. She closed the top drawer and opened another that contained photographs and newspaper clippings and handwritten letters.

Alice picked up a few of the photographs and shuffled through them like a card dealer looking to remove the Jokers from a rummy deck. Nothing in particular stood out, so she set them down and turned her attention to the letters written on brittle, yellowed paper. They were each dated at the top between 1912 and 1916. Someone had organized them chronologically and with alternating salutations: "My Sweetest Muriel"; "My Dearest Yuri." She gasped at her realization that she was holding 100-year-old love letters exchanged between Eliot's great-grandparents.

Her thoughts turned quickly to Joe, a hunched lurp with kind eyes whom she had never met, but had pieced together through the few stories that Eliot had told her. It seemed to her as if Joe had kept the letters with the hope of preserving the splendor of unadulterated love even as his own marriages were steadily failing. Alice collected a stack in her chilly hands and sat down on top of a wooden crate that she would later come to find contained Joe's record player, and read for hours.

She spent most of her time simply puzzling out the scrawl of Yuri's mangled handwriting, the result of arthritic cold, smashed bones, and general fatigue. Muriel's letters were significantly more legible, composed as they were of the smooth loops and unbroken strokes that signified a young girl's affection. The miracle of their love, Alice discovered in their contrasting penmanship, was not that they had encountered one another oceans from their native homes, but that they were able to survive the brutality of an immigrant's life in post-war America. *How did they do it,* she wondered, *what came after the* letters? Together Yuri and Muriel had prospered even as their city, this city, had crumbled all around them. And now, Alice found herself fenced in by the hallow artifacts of their love, including the boy with the pale-blue eyes from whom she could not escape.

So this is love, Alice thought as she measured the weight of the letters in her hands. She was pleased that they were heavy, substantial. Those letters bore the burden of a lifetime built upon a solid foundation of longing and hardship. *What was it Eliot had said of Cleveland, it's a place where you have to suffer for your love? Yes, that's it. Well,* she thought, *I've done my part.* Alice had given up her dream of living in Manhattan and moved to a dusty corner of Cleveland's near-East Side because she believed in the magic that had brought them together. She had even estranged herself from her parents, who both very much liked Eliot Hopkins, but not their daughter betraying her aspirations in order to be with him. As she closed her eyes a tear escaped and rolled down the soft ball of her cheek before splashing against the pile of notes in her hands. Wiping away the wet trail, Alice composed herself and returned the papers to their place in Joe's dresser drawer. She hadn't yet been able to begin seeing these things as hers, or even Eliot's. There were other chests to explore, but she had grown hungry and tired so she decided to make her way downstairs to wait for Eliot to arrive home.

In the kitchen, next to the sink, an arm's length from where her name was etched into the doorframe, she found a bunch of bananas hanging from a fruit hook and tore one away while the water she had set to boil upon the stove began to bubble. The banana was still slightly green, which she preferred to a perfectly ripe specimen both for flavor and consistency. The kettle whistled. Alice poured the steaming water over a tea bag draped over the edge of a coffee mug that Eliot had transferred from his dad's apartment. She scooped her index finger through the looped ceramic handle, scorching her knuckles against the hot mug, and snatched the banana from the counter on her way back into the amber glow of the living room.

Alice set her mug down on the box that she had previously been using as an ottoman, and placed the fruit next to it in the same motion that landed her askew on the couch. Her legs and doubly-stockinged feet tucked beneath her for added warmth as she gazed out through the drafty bay window that Eliot had not so long ago peered into, hoping to spy the very ghosts that Alice had discovered in the attic. She watched as the American Flyer silently speed around the track that Eliot had laid at the edge of the Christmas village with miniature railroad spikes and a tiny hammer. The mute, ceaseless pull of the engine reminded her of Lake View Cemetery, full of its soundless bones buried beneath white blankets—unseen and unseeing. She listened for the long-past clamor of the living, but even a life as remarkable as Yuri's could not pierce the void of death to animate this house. Alice allowed her eyelids to droop with the speed of gently falling snow as her body pressed heavily into the cushions. Before her eyes had fully closed a light gleamed forth from within the house across the street. Her mind raced toward Manhattan while the toy train stubbornly followed its eternal loop around the small Christmas village.

December

Forsaken
December 30, 2013

"WHAT ARE WE DOING HERE, FRANK?" Cornell asked his friend as he pushed Frank's wheelchair along a narrow and uneven section of sidewalk. They were headed from their parked car toward a line of weary-looking people waiting in-line alongside a mound of recently plowed snow.

"I've lived in this city for forty-two years, and I've never been here. I figured I might as well finally see the place before I leave it all behind for parts unknown," Frank said. Cornell stopped pushing the wheelchair long enough to clear away the small accumulation of snow that had built up around the wheels and was making it difficult to steer.

"We're not leaving forever. And the most exotic place we're going is Chicago, what do you mean 'parts unknown'?" Cornell said as he kicked at the snow. "And besides," he added before Frank had a chance to respond, "I've been living here longer than you, but you don't hear me bellyaching."

"Bellyaching is exactly what I hear! And I don't know why, you're the one who watched the movie at least ten times over the past month."

"There wasn't anything else on!"

"Sure, sure. Well, what else did you have planned for today that's so important?" Frank asked.

"Nothing," Cornell said begrudgingly. "But it's still colder than a coal-miner's ass out here!" He scooped snow out of his impractical winter shoes—a decade old pair of Adidas Sambas. "Damn it," he cursed, feeling a pool of thawed snow in his sock. "You'd think they'd at least clear the sidewalk with the amount of people they expect here every day. What's the price of admission cover, anyway?"

"I thought you said we were going to L.A.?"

"Huh?"

"The Papish Cats. Aren't you guys playing a couple of shows in L.A.?"

"Yeah. So?"

"And don't you think L.A. is just slightly more exotic than Chicago?" Frank asked his thoroughly frustrated friend.

"C'mon Frank. You know what I meant!"

Frank laughed heartily. "I'm just busting your balls, pal. Relax, this'll be a good send off—something to remind us that not everything in this town is worthless." He pointed toward a group of young men a few places ahead of them in line. They were about Eliot's age and all wore unnecessarily puffy Cleveland Browns coats. Frank was specifically referring to the team's recent loss to Pittsburgh, which not only ended the Browns's season with a seven game losing streak, but also gave the Steelers a chance to make the playoffs.

"Pitchers and catchers report to camp in forty-four days," Cornell said. It was his way of introducing a little bit of optimism into the conversation. "Tribe is still undefeated in 2014."

"Yeah." Frank had heard it before.

"I'm going to run across the street for tickets. You want anything? Coffee?" Cornell asked.

"Nah. I'm good."

Cornell trudged through the tree lawn where the snow had been piled almost to his knees. The small section of sidewalk directly in front of the museum had been carefully cleared into the patch of grass bordering the road. He stepped off the curb between two parked cars and waited for a break in the nearly uninterrupted traffic that slogged through the neighborhood. It seemed as if half the city had taken the day off to look at holiday decorations before they were removed after the New Year. Eventually he was able to dart between a rusted pickup and an SUV with out of state plates that had slowed enough for the kids in the back seats to realize that the building they had seen on television was a real place. To Cornell, their widened eyes were worth more than the price of admission.

When he finally reached the ticket booth on the other side of the street, he spied a small speaker beneath the transaction window that was playing the more memorable quotations from *A Christmas Story* on a maddeningly short loop. He hadn't spent more than five minutes waiting in the considerably shorter line than the entrance queue to the regionally-famous *Christmas Story* House across the street, but he had heard "You'll shoot your eye out!" at least a couple dozen times. While waiting, his thoughts had turned to the concluding sentence of Samuel Beckett's *The Unnamable* in mock despair: *"You must go on, I can't go on, I'll go on."* He planned to share the joke with Frank as he pocketed their tickets and set off back across the busy street.

Though it hadn't felt like it to him, the line for tickets appeared to have moved much faster than the admission queue in which Frank had been holding their place. When Cornell returned to the spot at which he had deposited his friend a few minutes earlier, he noticed that the wheelchair hadn't advanced a single inch from its original perch beneath the overhanging branches of a snow-covered tree, about thirty people from the entrance.

"Olive and I planned on coming here once. We were still in high school. Seniors. She ended up getting the flu. That turned out to be a pretty good day, anyhow," Frank remembered. Cornell knew not to interrupt him when he was talking about Olivia. It was best to let him enjoy the memory. "She loved Christmas," Frank continued, looking at the freshly painted yellow house trimmed with green accents. The large maple tree that stood in the Parker's front yard had been cut down, or fallen over, and a short wooden fence had been added to the perimeter of the yard, but it otherwise looked exactly as it had in the movie—even the stairs and roof were properly blanketed with snow.

The house next door, which in the movie had belonged to the Parker's "hillbilly neighbors," the Bumpuses, had been torn down to make room for additional parking on the overcrowded street. "We would drive down to the Terminal Tower and just walk around Public Square looking into the old Higbee's Department Store windows that were decorated for the season with scenes from the North Pole—all those mechanical elves working in their woodshops and playing in the snow. I was going to propose to her on Christmas day, up in New York, but she beat me to it," he smiled at the memory of his wife, and after clearing his throat continued, "I used to take Eliot downtown when he got older, before the accident, but it wasn't quite the same." He craned his neck to look at Cornell realizing that his memory might have seemed like an accusation. It wasn't. He never blamed his friend for the loss of his legs. Instead he would say that where he had lost his limbs he had gained an entire human being. He tried to steer Cornell's thoughts away from the accident: "I still haven't been to Cooperstown."

Cornell bobbed his head. The blue pom atop his old Indians knit cap bounced back-and-forth. It looked vaguely like those newer hats worn by a number of other people waiting in the idle line: a red cuff, the word *Cleveland* stitched across the front in white yarn. Cornell's was a relic of the 80s; the pom was its identifying feature.

Frank sighed and pulled a joint from his breast pocket. He sparked it, took a deep drag, and passed it to Cornell who did the same. The group of guys in their oversized Browns coats turned at the sweet smell of marijuana smoke, and each of them nodded his head in approval. They raised high their beer cans. One of them barked to show his approval, a habit that chronic tailgaters had trouble breaking beyond the context of a hopeful Sunday morning in the Municipal Parking Lot. Both men ignored the juvenile show of solidarity. Frank returned his gaze to the house, and Cornell snuffed the joint into the snow before pocketing it in time to push the wheelchair a few feet closer to the entryway.

Cornell, who was not only the founding member and bassist of the Papish Cats, but also their manager, had recently finished booking a tour of twenty U.S. Cities, including a stop in upstate New York to coincide with a visit to Cooperstown in July. He bought Frank tickets to the Hall of Fame induction ceremony. He hadn't yet told Frank, who just recently agreed to accompany the band as their soundboard operator since they planned to record a live album on the road. To keep himself from spilling the proverbial beans, Cornell occupied himself by hammering out a drum solo on the wheelchair's handles.

"Elvin Jones?" Frank asked after the drumming had gone on for a few bars.

"Close."

"Tony Williams?"

"Not quite. Here." Cornell sped up the rhythm and flicked at the exposed metal beneath the chair's rubber handles in order to add a steady cymbal crash.

"Billy Cobham," Frank said as soon as he heard the first *dwink* of fingernail against steel. He actually didn't know that it was a Billy Cobham beat, but by process of elimination (he had already guessed Cornell's top two favorite jazz drummers) it was the smartest choice.

"Right on," Cornell confirmed, impressed with Frank's ability to identify the rare solo. He maintained the beat while looking around at the faces of all the weary people waiting to enter the house. Those exiting it looked a little less tired. He was most interested in the group just milling about the area between the museum and gift shop unsure if they wanted to pay ten bucks to actually go inside when they could see the leg lamp from the street. Very few, if any, seemed excited to be there. He wondered if they felt some sort of obligation to experience this bright spot in an otherwise squalid town. He did, anyhow.

Frank, looking over the crowd from the same vantage point had come to a similar conclusion. Seeing so many of their fellow museumgoers leaning heavily against the fence or one another, some shifting uncomfortably from foot-to-foot, lead him to conclude aloud that, "In the world of stagnant lines the man with no legs is king."

His statement elicited no response from Cornell who was busy watching as people drove by and slowed their cars just enough to get a clear picture of the home's exterior, obviously focusing their lenses on the famous leg lamp illuminated in the wide front window. "Who needs the Lombardi Trophy, when you've got the lamp?" Cornell asked Frank. The boys in orange and brown had entered the house, leaving only a few more people between them and the door.

"Pffft. Some major award that is. You know you can buy those things at the drugstore?" The line was moving quickly now, and it was their turn to go in. The wheelchair ramp wound around the side of the porch, leading to a door near the back of the house. Frank and Cornell entered through the kitchen whereas most people began their tour in the living room. The house was tiny, smaller than Frank's apartment behind the bookstore, and narrower, too. There was also no way for him to get up the stairs to see the boys' bedroom or the shared bathroom—site of Ralphie's infamous *Little Orphan Annie* Decoder Ring letdown. They did a quick loop of the ground floor and snuck out the back door from which they had entered.

"That was a total waste of twenty bucks," Cornell said.

"Yeah, sorry. I owe you," Frank admitted.

"You want to at least swing through the gift shop? I gotta take a leak."

"Sure." They rolled across the street toward the ticket window and the loud speaker now broadcasting the fairly racist version of "Deck the Halls" sung by a troop of Chinese Restaurant workers. No one seemed to mind.

Once they arrived inside, though, their mood changed instantly. The place buzzed with the excitement of post-Christmas sale prices, and people joyously spending a couple hundred dollars on replica leg lamps, Red Ryder BB guns, and assorted housewares.

What caught Frank's eye, however, was a second room set off from the main store, and dedicated to a very different Christmas story, one much dearer to his own heart: *National Lampoon's Christmas Vacation*. He wheeled himself directly into the center of that room where a small model neighborhood was set up. There was the Griswold house, Cousin Eddie's RV tucked into the driveway and Clark standing among the tangle of electrical cords prepared to light the house. "Would you look at that," he instructed Cornell. "I think I just might have to buy this for Eliot…for the platform."

"It doesn't really match the rest of the pieces," Cornell pointed out.

"Who says it has to match? Eliot will get a kick out of this! Plus, I want to get him something really nice, considering—"

"Yeah, I guess you probably should. I can't believe you haven't said anything yet."

"I'll tell him tonight."

"Nothing like waiting until the last minute."

Frank grabbed one of the boxed from the pile that had been arranged to look like a Christmas Tree next to the display model and heaved it onto his lap. "This is such a better movie," he said to Cornell, ignoring his friend's disapproval.

"I don't know man, *A Christmas Story* is pretty hilarious."

"Every tragedy is a comedy, unless you're the victim," Frank quipped.

"I suppose that's right."

"Okay, we should get out of here. I have to swing by the pet store on the way back to the shop to pick up a bag of dog food, and I want to make sure that I see Eliot before he has a chance to make dinner plans. I'm gonna ask if he wants to drive down to Brother's Lounge with me tonight for the gig."

They navigated their way through the crowded store toward the registers where Frank spent a good sum of money on his gift for Eliot. He even sprung the extra five dollars to have it wrapped, which cost them a few extra minutes while the cashier covered the box in holiday paper and expertly furled ribbons between her thumb and scissors. When she was done, the two made their way toward the door being held open as a man stood outside taking one last drag from the stump of his cigarette. Once he saw them approaching, he flicked the filter into the street and continued holding the door ajar for them to more easily exit.

"Hey, Mike," Frank said to the man as they passed through the open door.

"Oh! Hey, Frank," Mike coughed. He hadn't recognized either of them outside the usual context of the bookstore. He acknowledged Cornell with a nod. "What are you guys up to?" He asked once he recovered from the small coughing fit. Mike had been a pretty steady customer at Big Sleep Books for the past few years, sustaining his hankering for Elmore Leonard novels and conversation, but Frank had never seen him smoke before. He was a small-change ambulance chaser who had moved to Shaker Heights for no discernible reason after completing his law degree at La Roche College in Pittsburgh, leading Frank to assume he didn't have very many friends. But he was a nice guy, and both Frank and Cornell kind of enjoyed his weekly visits to the shop, especially when he would share stories about what he had seen in the area's surrounding emergency rooms.

"We just finished taking the tour." Cornell said, jabbing his thumb toward the house. "How about you, we haven't seen you around the store for a few weeks."

"I've been busy, and then out of town with the holidays and all." It was a partial lie. He had visited his sister in Pittsburgh for Thanksgiving, but he was really covering up the fact that he had started purchasing many of his books online— mostly for the convenience of not having to leave the house in the cold, but also because they were just insanely cheap.

"You coming or going?" Frank asked.

"Oh, I'm headed in next. I was just going to stop in here for a few minutes to warm up and to buy a bag of those roasted chestnuts. Hey, did you guys see Ian Petrella?" Mike said.

"Who's that?" Frank asked.

"Ian Petrella, he's the actor who played Randy. You know, 'I can't put my arms down!" Mike shot his own fat arms out from his sides, making himself into a stout T. "I guess he lives in the house now. He gives tours."

"Bummer," Frank said, struck by the woeful circumstance of a man so trapped by his singular accomplishment that he literally inhabits the past.

"No way, it's awesome," Mike said.

"Maybe for you, but it's gotta suck for him. Can you imagine how many times per day somebody probably asks him to show them how the little piggy eats?" Frank said.

"Hell yeah! I was gonna ask him for sure," Mike said, finally lowering his arms back to his sides.

"He's a grown-ass man, Mike," Cornell pointed out. "It's not gonna be the same anymore."

"Whatever," Mike said. "Listen, it was good running into you guys. Happy Holidays and all that. I'll see you at the store after the New Year." He moved to squeeze around Frank's chair, but Frank remained still.

"I'm actually not going to be around next year, but you should still come by. Eliot's taking over."

"Retiring already?"

"I just have to get out of town for a bit, hit the reset button. Maybe see something before it's too late," Frank explained.

"Man, I hear that," Mike agreed. "So the store must be doing well," he said in part to temper his feeling of guilt for not giving Frank his business.

"Not exactly. Eliot's been kicking in to help keep the doors open. It's a team effort these days. But, uh, I was able to sock away a bit of travel money to help out with Cornell's tour. The Papish Cats are recording a live album, so I'm gonna run the soundboard for them. Save them a few bucks and see some sights at the same time."

"Oh Yeah?" Mike said to Cornell.

"Mhmm, we're gonna do something like forty shows in nine months and then birth this record," Cornell said.

"Cool. Are you guys playing any Cleveland shows?"

"Yeah, man. We kick things off tonight at Brother's Lounge on Detroit Ave. You should come out, bring a couple friends." Cornell suggested. "I can put you on the list."

"What list?" Mike asked.

"To get you in for free. Like, you're with the band," Cornell explained. "We don't get paid based on admission, just a cut of the bar, so come thirsty."

"Oh, cool! Yeah, maybe I'll swing by—if the weather's not too bad. I think it's supposed to really come down tonight."

"All right, Mike," Cornell said, disappointed that he obviously wasn't planning to come to the show.

"Hey, good luck, guys. And I'll definitely get a copy of your CD when it comes out," he lied.

"Thanks, Mike. Take it easy," Frank said, and wheeled himself down the ramp to the uneven, snow-covered sidewalk where Cornell took over.

"Could that guy be any less cool?" Cornell asked Frank once they were almost back to the car.

"I doubt it," Frank said, lifting himself into the driver's seat. Once he was situated, Cornell folded up his chair and placed it in the trunk before sliding into the car and cranking on the heater.

"Let's roll, I'm starving."

* * *

Eliot awoke on the floor of Big Sleep Books that morning wearing an old pair of jeans and a faded Dead Boys T-shirt. His mouth was dry and his feet were bare; at some point during the night he had tied a red scarf around his neck. His glasses, amazingly, had remained on his face during his slumber on the hardwood, making his transition to consciousness a little less hazy. He was spooning Dillinger. Eliot glanced at his watch as he raised his arms past his face for a stretch. He noted that it was 8:45 AM, and upon completing his stretch, he pushed his hand through his hair and hopped to his feet amidst the debris of a partially demolished wall.Eliot had moved the Great Dane's futon against the front window display the previous day, ensuring that the dog would remain mostly out of the way and able to nap in the late-afternoon sun. Now, his own bones ached from having slept on the hard floor. He recalled turning off the radio and lying down for a moment to rest his eyes, which apparently had become a full night's sleep. "So it goes," he said in homage to Vonnegut. This was his usual response to life's smaller errors.

He shook out the stiffness in his joints and peered into the pallid morning as he flipped open the steel lock on the front door and turned the sign from *closed* to *open*. A thin layer of frost covered everything in his field of vision. It looked painfully cold, and he hoped that the dog, who had relocated to the comfort of the futon, would sleep for another hour or two before asking to go out.

Eliot switched on the lights. The shop was quiet, and for a few moments the low buzz of the overhead fluorescent tubes heating up was the only sound that filled the room. Looking out onto the barren street, he recalled the conversation he had had with his father the previous evening about working at the store full-time, which had resulted in Eliot taking a sledgehammer to the wall.

Pat Murphy had stopped by to drop off a thoughtful, but meager, Christmas bonus and to apologetically deliver the news that the electric company had to lay Eliot off for the remainder of the winter now that the sidewalk lamps had all been installed at John Carroll and there was no remaining work on the books. "Business is slow," he had said, looking around the empty bookstore, "You understand." It had seemed like an insult, but Pat was simply describing the general state of things across Northeast Ohio the past few years.

It was when Pat had left and Eliot sat contemplating his future that he remembered Alice's suggestion: *"You should open a coffee shop."* It wasn't a bad idea. He would be spending more time at the bookstore anyhow, and he definitely had a wide-ranging knowledge of coffee. With a small investment of time and money, both of which he had, Eliot could conceivably build a successful coffee bar. A few hours after her initial suggestion, Eliot had reworked her idea as an addition to the business he already kind of owned, or at least planned to inherit. Perhaps with a little elbow grease Big Sleep Books & Coffee Traders wouldn't suffer the fate of Vern's gas station and the rotting shell of his '68 Cutlass Supreme.

The Gulf Station had become a routine stop for Eliot at least once per week on his drive between the bookstore and his house on E. 74th, and the sight of that car on its pedestal of cinder blocks depressed him every time he saw it. He had asked once if Vern was looking to sell it, and was more than relieved when he said no. Eliot didn't really want to buy it, but he wanted the old man to realize he had something enviable if he would only put in the hours, and, admittedly, the significant amount of money it would take to restore it.

Eliot had spent the previous evening exposing the building's century-old plumbing, which he now studied. Everything seemed to be in good order, which to Eliot meant nothing was actively leaking—repairing pipes was the one trade he had never picked up. But he could now more easily see the previously hidden potential of the small corner tucked beneath the stairs that lead to the bargain loft. He stepped his feet into his shoes, which he found lying near a small pile of tools and contorted his arms behind his back so that he could scratch an itch that had settled in between his shoulder blades. Once satisfied, he yanked the scarf from his neck and, leaning against the counter, stared at the mess. His memory began to finally wake up, following all the cues of his reluctant body, and he frowned at the hole in the wall that reflected hole in his heart. "Damn it," Eliot swore at the hole and Alice.

From atop the counter, he scooped up a full-page printout of the used espresso machine he had purchased online at

Alice's suggestion. He hung his head at the thought of her absence. She had graduated a few days ago, a semester early. He didn't attend the commencement ceremony. Afterwards, she moved back to Buffalo with her parents. They had convinced her, he told himself, to begin the M.F.A. program at New York University in the spring. Though she had signed her name on the wooden post in his kitchen, Alice left. He knew that she possessed too much talent to remain in Cleveland with the likes of him, but had hoped she wouldn't realize it. He was being unfair, but so was life.

Eliot held the page up to block the demolished wall and the memory of Alice Browne, and vaguely recalled the layout of Third Rail Coffee—the small shop he and Alice and Nick visited on their enchanted tour of New York City's West Village. He appreciated the shop's simplicity and planned to replicate it inside the unassuming bookstore his father had acquired on Coventry Road in 1999, long after Lou Reed and Patti Smith had autographed the walls in the early 70s. The celebrity had faded along with their signatures, and nothing was going to bring it back. Eliot turned his attention to brewing his own cup of coffee using a hot plate that he had relocated from the apartment's kitchen sometime during Adam and Andy's radio show the previous evening—meaning he had been awake until at least 2:00 AM listening to punk rock and fart jokes: a feeble attempt at lifting his spirits.

He turned on the radio, still tuned to WJCU, and waited for the water to boil. An Iggy and the Stooges song bled through the speakers, and he punched the volume button a few times until it blared. Though he had opened the store, no one would come for a few hours, and even then the first couple people through the door would only want to know if they could use the toilet. Mondays were typically slow, and the Monday between Christmas and New Year's Eve was always a total bust. So in the meantime, he squawked along with Iggy's gnarled howl and angrily strummed at his air guitar while the coffee brewed: "I am the world's forgotten boy, the one who searches and destroys. Honey gotta help me please! Somebody gotta save my soul! Baby detonates for me!" Eliot couldn't tell if the music jived with his mood or influenced it, and he didn't care. He was frustrated, angry, in the middle of a massive life change that had been forced upon him with the news that he was out of a construction job, and Alice Browne's abrupt exit. Despite his irritation, though, he did feel, for the first time in a long while, like he was directing his own life—a circumstance that, regrettably, almost no one that he knew personally had ever experienced. It was both mightily unsettling and deeply satisfying.

With Alice gone and no trenches to dig in ice-encrusted grounds, Eliot would sell books and sling coffee with his dad and best friend. He owned a house, and was improving his business. Eliot could not go back to digging holes and pulling wire after the spring thaw. He had had enough of that life, and if he couldn't bring himself to abandon Cleveland, at the very least he could escape its trenches. Alice had helped to convince him of that. At times it had seemed as if she cared about his happiness far more than he did. She also possessed the uncanny ability to convince him that he deserved something better than what he had been dealt, which is why after only a month of dating he had asked Alice Browne to marry him.

At the time she had said yes. And then the phone rang: she was moving to New York. Alice attempted to explain that the program would only take her two years to complete, and that she loved him immensely. They could make it work! She seemed almost desperate, as if her hand had been forced and the decision to leave him hadn't been her decision at all. But if she wasn't willing to fight, then Eliot wasn't so sure that they could make it work. Ultimately, he felt betrayed. More, he was certain that the lure of Manhattan would be too powerful for her to escape once she became attuned to the vibrations of The City.

His eyes scanned the long expanse of the narrow store overgrown with the small forests that his father had been unable to sell. There was a particularly delicate swaddle that made him feel comfortable—warm in spite of the frigid winter nipping at the windows. He sucked in the smells of coffee and the sounds of freedom. Everything he loved was not only associated with, but built into that space: a quiet reading corner in the basement, Dillinger wandering about the shelves, jive talking with Cornell, listening to baseball games on the radio with his dad…everything except Alice.

He forced his mind away from her memory once again: *Maybe I should add a beer tap instead of the coffee bar so that we can have a pint during Indians games this summer.* Eliot imagined how he and Frank would throw open the front door on a humid July evening to let the ambient sounds of the neighborhood waft indoors: idling motorcycle engines, the purr of endless conversation fragments and drunken declarations.

His water had reached a boil. He removed the kettle from the hotplate and set it aside. Eliot looked into the empty mug he had used last night, and, judging it acceptably clean, unfurled a paper filter and tucked it into his V-60, which he set on the mug's rim. He then scooped a generous heap of ground coffee from its tall paper bag into the filter and saturated the grounds with water from the kettle. The concoction trickled into his mug, unseen.

The speed of this process had always intrigued Eliot: the alchemy of turning water and ground-up bean dust into a muddy elixir that told a story of the place and the people who had cultivated the exotic plant. The French called that story of place *terroir*—at least according to the *sommelier* that worked the late shift at La Cav Du Vin, the subterranean wine bar located a long block north of Big Sleep Books. The *sommelier* had a 'thing' for Eliot (if Cornell's sense of things was to be trusted, and they usually were). Eliot liked stories, and he liked that his cup of coffee had one to tell. And in many ways, he reasoned, it was his story—a love affair that had allowed him to travel the world through his senses when he didn't have the fortitude to venture too far from home. Though he had tried, Eliot's humble imagination could not conceive of the care that went into picking the ripe cherries, or the precision of raking the sun-dried fruit. Those tasks are the very opposite of a quality he knew too well: apathy. The current of his paltry life was affected by the social miracle of this vulnerable fruit, so were the grander narratives of the human condition.

He savored the first slurp from his mug—a bittersweet memoir of Ethiopia's Yirgacheffe District and the inescapable essence of Alice. He set the mug down on the bookshop counter in order to turn his full attention to the antique church pew he had salvaged from the Cabinet of Curiosities on Erie Street in Willoughby—the same shop from which Frank had purchased the red cash register more than a decade earlier. Alice had pointed out the pew a couple weeks after they had returned from New York, suggesting they purchase it to use as bench seating on one side of their kitchen table in the new house. Now that Eliot had decided to build a coffee bar in the bookstore, he thought it appropriate to destroy the relic of their domestic partnership that had lasted less than a single month. Plus, the pew perfectly captured the tenor of the project: a Hail Mary designed to save an obsolete business. He set to work removing the polished-oak pew back from its legs; the pounding captured a few stares from passers-by, but no one entered the shop.

It wasn't long before he heard the back door slam shut at the far end of the apartment, signaling the return of Frank and Cornell from their mysterious 'holiday outing.' Dillinger, who hadn't moved since Eliot awoke, except to relocate from the floor to the futon cushion, stood up and began scratching his shoulder with his back leg. It both looked and sounded like the driver rods on a steam locomotive. The motion seemed to propel the big black dog forward as the scratching turned into an all out sprint toward the slam of the door, claws skittering with excitement across the hardwood floors. Eliot felt a pang of guilt for not waking the dog to take him outside or to feed him breakfast, but he was old and uninterrupted sleep seemed more important. The back door slammed a second time, signaling that Cornell was kindly attending to Eliot's oversight. A moment later, Frank rolled through the door behind the counter, still wearing his hat and gloves and overcoat.

"So, where'd you guys go?" Eliot asked without looking up from his work. He was attaching the pew to the base he had built that morning.

Wanting to retain the surprise of his gift, Frank didn't immediately answer the question. "Wow, you've made a lot of progress, kid. It looks great!"

"Thanks. The real work will be hooking up the hot water lines as soon as the espresso machine arrives, which should be in a day or two. We still have to work out the merch."

Frank nodded to signal that he was impressed.

"I was thinking we could custom design a few dozen Big Sleep mugs to have on hand here, and maybe we can come up with a stamp or something for to-go cups. Mobile marketing."

"You've thought of everything, huh?" Frank said.

"I've done a lot of research over the years without really knowing I was doing research."

"Sounds promising. I think you're doing a good thing here," Frank said.

"Slinging coffee is a lot like selling books."

"Caffeine and mystery. We're drug dealers," Frank proclaimed.

"We're gonna be all right, pop," Eliot said to his dad who had turned an apprehensive eye toward the hole that had appeared in the wall overnight.

"What about that?" he pointed to the exposed pipes.

"A little angst therapy, I guess," Eliot said. "I'll be able to close that up even before the machine gets here. I'm going to run an access line across the floor and into the bar then patch and paint it. I should have that done by tomorrow at the latest. Probably tonight."

"Alice doesn't mind you spending all your free time at the shop?" Frank asked.

Eliot retrieved his coffee from the counter and gave it his full attention. She had already been in Buffalo for two days and he hadn't yet told his father the news. He supposed it was time.

"Alice left." It was the first time he had said it aloud, and the words almost caught in his throat. He couldn't even bring himself to look Frank in the eye when he said it, as if it were his fault, that he had somehow failed.

"Oh?" Frank asked. "What about you?"

"I'm fine," he lied.

"Yeah, but are you going, too? I mean, what about the store?"

"Thanks a bunch, pop."

"Eliot, you know what I mean. Obviously I'm sorry you two broke up…did you break up?"

"Not entirely. I don't know. It's complicated," Eliot said as he worked out the question in his own mind.

"These things always are," Frank assured him.

Eliot took his father's comment as invitation to vent about what was really bothering him: "We can't all just abandon this place, right? If nobody sticks around to make it a home, then it will never be one. I've got a life here, and you and CT. I don't really want to try to make it in New York. You know? Maybe some people just like the Midwest."

"Yeah, I get it," Frank said, increasingly ashamed that he was abandoning the place, to use Eliot's words. "Look, kiddo...."

"Plus, fuck the Yankees."

Frank laughed.

"Anyway, her program is only two years. Maybe we can do the long-distance thing, and when it's all over she'll move back," Eliot added. Then he thought better of his optimism, "Probably not. This isn't really one of those 'next year' scenarios."

Frank shrugged in agreement, and said. "Eliot, bud, I don't want you to feel like the whole world is abandoning you here––"

"I don't—"

"But I'm taking off for a little bit, too."

"What!? Where to?" Eliot asked, exasperated. His eyes closed and his shoulders hunched beneath the weight of it all.

"With Cornell," Frank explained. "When I agreed to go I thought that Alice was going to be here, that you'd have some help with the store. A life."

"Are you going for the whole tour?"

"That is the plan."

He opened his eyes and looked at Frank: "And when were you planning on telling me? What if I had electrical work? What if I wanted to go with Alice? I couldn't do any of that now! But I guess you could count on me to have absolutely no prospects."

"It's not like that."

"No? What's it like, Dad?" Eliot turned away from Frank and looked around the bookstore, letting his fate sink in. He would be a prisoner to these white walls for the next year, from sunup to sundown, and then some. There's no way he'd be able to get away on weekends or for holidays to visit Alice in Manhattan. And she's not going to want to travel all the way to

Cleveland on her breaks to work a double selling pulp fiction to Frank's loyal customers: guys he went to high school with and the handful of readers in Cleveland Heights who weren't complete burnouts.

Then it dawned on him. "Shit," Eliot murmured. Frank had been that lonely prisoner for the past fourteen years. He deserved, perhaps more than anyone, an opportunity to see something new.

"So when do you guys leave?" Eliot asked, embarrassed by his outburst.

"The tour kicks off tonight at Brother's," Frank said. "We were hoping you'd come down."

"That's tonight?! With everything happening, I completely forgot. What time do they go on?"

"Nine thirty," Cornell interjected. He had just come in the front door with Dillinger, who he let off the leash so that the dog could inspect Frank before returning to his bed. "Everything cool?" He asked, eyeing Frank.

"Man, you should have told me," Eliot said to Cornell, his anger refocused on the fact that both men had kept this a secret from him.

"Not my place, Ness," Cornell said, looking at the wall. "What the hell did you do to the wall?"

"Alice left," Frank said.

Cornell raised his eyebrows at Eliot as if that didn't entirely explain the demolition.

"I'm putting in a coffee bar. Trying to drum up some more business. I'll have the wall patched up by tomorrow afternoon."

Cornell scrunched up his face and nodded his head. He ran his hand along the newly installed bar top, and rapping them against the edge a few times to test its durability. "I dig the understated blasphemy," he said, choosing to ignore, for the moment, the loss of Alice Browne from their lives.

"I thought you'd like that," Eliot said, and cracked a wide smile.

"So, when do we open for business?" Cornell asked.

"Probably about a week," Eliot said. He then turned to Frank and said, "I was actually thinking about putting in a tap so we could have draught beers this summer while we listen to Tribe games. We couldn't sell them without a liquor license, but it'd be fun to throw back a few cold ones ourselves."

"Mmm," Frank sounded his approval.

"Anyway, maybe the Tribe will make the playoffs and we can tap an Octoberfest when you guys get back. I'm gonna miss you two."

Frank smiled at the boy he had raised to love the Indians and Budweiser, "That's for sure!" He hated that he had to leave his son. Not only because they would miss the entire 2014 season, but also because he knew that he couldn't afford to hire anyone to help out at the shop, and that Alice wouldn't be visiting while working toward her degree. Frank knew writers: they needed solitude, time to think—a room of one's own he remembered Olivia telling him before she turned the spare bedroom in their small house on Nicholas Avenue into her office. "Hey! I got you something!" Frank remembered.

Eliot's phone rang. He looked at the screen and saw it was Alice. Her name on his screen flashed with the weight of a sack of concrete. "Sorry, I've got to take this. Do you mind?"

"No, go ahead," Frank said, disappointment tugging at his lips.

"Cool. Are you guys around for the afternoon if I take off for a bit?" The phone rang a second time.

"I'm headed out to get things packed up for the gig, but your dad will be here," Cornell said.

"You okay here for a little while? I was going to walk down The Hill." Eliot said.

Frank waved him off, "You go. I'll be fine. I'll see you tonight at the club." The digital ring of Eliot's phone faded as he passed through the door with a quick wave goodbye.

Frank watched as Eliot quickly disappeared from the frame of the store's display windows. He looked concerned, if not hopeful, and Frank wondered what was on his mind. He was still staring out the window in the direction Eliot had vanished when Cornell asked him if he was sure he wanted to leave home for the better part of a year. "Yeah," Frank responded. "I've got to get out of here for a little while—for both of us. Eliot needs some space to do his own thing."

"Trial by fire" Cornell said.

"He needs something of his own. This is a good first step," he pointed to the newly installed coffee bar. "I just want him to worry about himself more than me. Maybe he'll realize that he should move to New York instead of being marooned in here with a cripple."

"C'mon Frank, you've never talked like that before," Cornell said to his friend.

"I'm just making a point. Look, it's not like I don't benefit from this tour, too. I've never been west of the Mississippi…or east of the Susquehanna for that matter. It'll be nice to have something to look forward to when I wake up in the morning." He paused for a moment to remember his wife. "I owe it to Olive. She always had that look of abandon in her eyes, like she was constantly scanning the horizon for an adventure. I guess I'm ready to see the world the way she did when we were kids playing among the branches of that old Willow tree in her backyard."

* * *

Eliot answered the phone. "Hi, Sweetest," he said out of habit, instantly regretting the salutation.

"Hi, Eliot" Alice said. "Are you busy?"

"No. I'm just walking to Presti's." He shoved one arm through his coat and hugged the phone between his ear and shoulder while he struggled the other arm into place. "I finished installing the bar this morning. It looks really good." Eliot turned left out of the store, traveling down Coventry Road past Tommy's Restaurant and Big Fun, the vintage toy store where he used to buy Star Wars action figures and back issues of *Mad Magazine* for a dollar. His long stride carried him swiftly past the bohemian storefronts decorating the west side of the street.

"That's great, Eliot. Are you done for the day?" She asked. The formality of her voice clued him into the fact that she was likely calling with news that he would not enjoy.

"Maybe. I've got some stuff lined up for this afternoon, and then I'm going to catch the Papish Cats tonight." He left out the part about his dad also electing to leave him.

"Where's that?"

"Westside." He turned left down Mayfield Road toward the cemetery. There was a break in the traffic so he gripped the phone tight against his ear and sprinted across the four-lane street that always reminded him of the rush of adrenaline that had overtaken his small frame when he had crossed it for the first time by himself. He was twelve years old then, and riding atop a squat Huffy mountain bike heading for the trails of Lake View Cemetery. The light was red when he started out on his own for the first time, but he had mistimed the crossing and an impatient series of cars bore down on him before he had pedaled even halfway across that unfamiliar expanse of asphalt. The horn blasts were deafening.

Now, Eliot imagined that Alice's doomed fawn had experienced a similarly unenviable bout of terror, and it occurred to him how lucky he had been to survive such a precarious route. "So, what's up?"

"Nothing. I was just wondering what the rest of your day looked like," Alice said. "We rented a U-Haul. My mom and I were going to drive down to get the rest of my stuff from the house."

"Oh." Eliot said. Alice's mother would arrive with a U-Haul to rescue her daughter from an irrelevant life—something his grandmother hadn't done for his mother. Eliot had finally begun to feel less guilty about asking her to abandon her dream of writing in New York City in order to live with him on the outskirts of Cleveland when she told him that she was leaving. Things had been progressing nicely; they were engaged. And then she was gone. Somehow the abandoned accouterments of her life had helped ease the shock of her absence.

"Are you heading back home afterwards, or are you pulling another all-nighter at the store?"

"I think I'd like to sleep in a bed tonight." Eliot stretched his back to see if the stiffness had yet subsided. It hadn't.

"You should," Alice instructed. "Anyway, it's a three hour drive, and it should only take us an hour or two to pack up." She paused for a long moment before asking, "Do you want us to wait for you?"

"Um. You can if you want." Eliot was unsure how to answer, unsure too if he was ready to see Alice or not. "I mean, I'm not entirely sure what we're doing yet, you and me, and I don't know if we want to try to hash it out with your mom there."

"That makes sense," She said. "I do love you, Eliot. I just have to do this."

"I know."

"I'll be back before you know it. Two years is not a long time." He could tell that she didn't believe her own words, and that she was perhaps about to cry before she changed the subject: "Have you at least been reading anything good while there's no one around to bother you?" She asked with a forced laugh.

Eliot had reached the top of Murray Hill and began his steady decline into the Italian neighborhood he had frequented so many times for street carnivals, art walks, concerts, and espresso. "Yeah, actually. I've gotten into a collection of First World War poetry that Joe left behind. I found it inside a pair of boots he left in the crawlspace beneath the stairs to the cellar," Eliot said, adding with an almost sacrosanct reverence, "It's beautifully sad."

"Just what you've been looking for," Alice said.

"Almost. I haven't gotten vey deep into it yet, and still no tears." He reminded her of his futile attempts to find a book that could make him cry. He presumed that real life had simply delivered on too many occasions.

"He really left behind an entire life," Alice said, referring to Joseph Kowalski Sr.

"He did. It's almost as if the house has taken ownership of its favorite things that people have brought into it over the years."

"Maybe I should leave something behind."

Eliot ignored her attempt at good will: "When I was in the cellar the other day I unearthed a crate of old wine bottles that look to me like they outdate even Joe."

"You should do something with them, like make a chandelier or a flower box," Alice suggested. Eliot would very much missed having her creative tendencies influence the way he interpreted the world. To Alice everything had a purpose. It was as if her mind installed a gilded picture frame around the objects of her perception, even century-old garbage, in order to put it on display for the world to appreciate.

Eliot missed waking up to the sound of her soft snore, and, once out of bed, following in reverse the long trail of discarded clothing she would have left from the front room to the bedroom the night before. He missed the intoxicating smells of various washes and lotions. Mostly, he missed listening to her type. He had actually bought her a housewarming present after watching her admire it in a second hand store, and planned to give it to her when she returned to Cleveland after the New Year.

The two of them had decided against exchanging Christmas presents since they were in the process of rehabilitating the house. Eliot reasoned that the piece was a home improvement, and splurged on an antique Royal Standard No. 5 typewriter that had caught her eye at The Cabinet of Curiosities in Willoughby while they were buying the church pew he just that morning repurposed as a coffee bar. When Eliot dropped the noisy machine at Ohio Typewriter Restoration in Rocky River, the repair technician who had seen as many years on this earth as the typewriters he lovingly restored to working order, instructed him to pick up the No. 5 "in a fortnight," which happened to be the very afternoon upon which he found himself strolling down The Hill toward Presti's Bakery.

Alice broke a comfortable, though perhaps too-long silence: "I'm planning a trip back to Cleveland in March to meet with a couple of professors about acquiring an agent and maybe picking up some freelance contracts."

"That sounds good. Hopefully I'll see get to see you," he said, forgetting that he hadn't yet told Alice that Frank was leaving and that he'd likely be stuck at the store.

"Well, that's the point," Alice said, and added worriedly, "Eliot, are we okay?"

"Yeah, sure. This is just a lot to process is all," Eliot said.

"I know. Well, maybe I'll just get my stuff from the house and then we can talk later, after you've had a chance to sort things out."

"That's probably best. Listen, I've got to run, but I'll call you," Eliot said.

"Okay," Alice said, audibly upset. Before she could finish Eliot had disconnected the call and proceeded down The Hill.

"Goddamn it," Eliot swore aloud as he shoved the phone into the breast pocket of his overcoat and turned his collar up against the cold. He thought about Alice's signature scratched into his doorframe like Hester Prynne's scarlet letter.

Eliot peered into the restaurants' darkened windows, but could see only the reflection of cars passing behind him on the street. He didn't slow his step, and quickly passed the Mayfield Smoke Shop and Mama Santa's Pizzeria. All around him were the remnants of the distant past: buildings that had outlived by generations the people who had built them.

The sweet smell of Corbo's Cassata cake met him as he crossed over E. 123rd Street. He noticed the line of cars that he saw reflected in the windows had come to a stop further down the hill. They idled along the curb in front of Presti's Bakery: a pair of 1956 Cadillac Coup de Villes, one the color of Elvis Presley's blue suede shoes, the other a bright-red Maraschino cherry, and a 1953 sea-foam green Oldsmobile Ninety-Eight. They were the type of cars you'd expect to see lining the streets in mid-August during the Feast of the Assumption, not a merciless January afternoon. A man dressed in all black appeared from a subterranean alcove at the side of Holy Rosary Catholic Church, and attached a small purple flag to the roof each automobile.

Eliot entered the bakery to the jangle of sleigh bells hanging from the door. He scuffed his soles along the all weather mat and stomped twice before testing his footing on the tile.

"Hey! Eliot?" a girl's voice called out. As was the case in the bookstore on Coventry, there was no line prohibiting Eliot from approaching the counter, so he had made it halfway to the cash register before stopping to look in the direction from which his name had been spoken as a question. One table, in the far-off corner of the café, and near the plate-glass window that allowed him to see the line of vintage cars still waiting for their escort, was occupied by a group of three college-aged girls, none of which Eliot recognized. He held up his hand to wave 'hello,' confirming his name as Eliot.

One of the girls, the one who looked simultaneously surprised and pleased that he responded to her call, waved him over to the table. She wore a red coat that matched her lips and the '56 Cadillac parked outside. Her black hair was tied up menacingly tight with a white ribbon, and her dark eyes dispatched a message that he couldn't decode. The crazy pattern of her stockings working against the altogether different crazy pattern of her skirt was troublesome, but Eliot was drawn to her. He immediately and foolhardily set off across the room toward the thin line of her smile.

"Hi," he said, unsure of what might be gained from this encounter. She was fiercely beautiful, and for the first time he understood the expression, 'a knockout.' Eliot felt woozy.

"Hi. I'm Kate," she said, raising a single eyebrow expectantly. When Eliot said nothing she added, "Alice's roommate."

Eliot's felt ashamed at the mention of Alice's name, as if the incantation allowed her to see his attraction to Kate. "Oh, Hey," Eliot said. "Sorry, I've never actually seen you in person. I mean, I've seen you in pictures, in the room. Uh, it's nice to meet you." It occurred to Eliot at that moment that his love for Alice had protected him from Kate's insidious allure.

"Right. This is weird." She held her fingers to her face in feigned embarrassment.

Eliot could tell that she wasn't actually embarrassed, but she was slightly awkward in an endearing sort of way. "Not at all," he assured her.

"I've seen you in pictures, too. Some of Alice's, from New York mostly. Anyway, I recognized you when you came in. Um, this is Sarah, and Natalie." The other girls smiled, but otherwise appeared disinterested. Eliot smiled back, though he hadn't taken his eyes off Kate. "Listen," she continued, "Alice left behind some stuff in our room when she moved out, and since she's officially graduated, I thought you might be able to stop by and pick it up? It's like some books and an electric kettle. I think a book. I was just gonna hang onto it until I saw her, but you should swing by. If you want."

Eliot recalled the books he had lent Alice, and the few small appliances he had brought over to ease the burden of dorm living. He wasn't prepared to get into a conversation about the fact that those were his things, or that he and Alice weren't really seeing each other at the moment, so he just nodded his head.

"The dorms aren't technically open during break. A few students have special permission to stay on campus. Mostly us science geeks who can't bring our senior projects home," Kate pointed at the other two girls. "I'm running experiments in the Bio-Chem lab, so I was able to get special permission to stay in Campion. I think I'm the only one though. These two live in Sutowski."

"146," one of the other girls said, as if it mattered.

"Okay. Does it have to be today, though? I actually have plans out on the west side the rest of the day."

"Stop by afterward," Kate suggested.

"It might be late."

"That's fine."

"I guess I can make it work. Is eleven, eleven-thirty okay?"

"Perfect," she said, and wrote down her cell phone number on the maroon bakery napkin. When she handed it to Eliot the tips of her fingers touched his palm.

"So, I'll just call when I get there?"

"I'll see you later." It was more command than confirmation, and her friends watched Eliot to see how he would respond.

He nodded obediently then left the girls and headed back toward the front counter where he would order an almond milk cappuccino and chat up the barista about their coffee beans and the brand of non-dairy milk they use for making espresso drinks. Eliot pulled his wallet and a small cardboard notebook from his back pocket. He paid the barista with cash and left a sturdy tip in the half-empty jar. Eliot scrawled some notes on a page that contained a sketch of a coffee cup with Alice's name written above it in steam. He then turned to take a seat at the counter running along the front window. He noted that Kate and her friends had left, and that he was alone in the café.

Outside, crowds of people filed into the vintage cars idling against the curb, filling the snow-capped neighborhood with white exhaust that swirled like a poison gas upon the Western Front. Eliot watched as they rolled away, one after another, following the curtained back window of the hearse. Behind their wheels, old men set their jowls and focused somber eyes upon the enviable shine of the chrome bumper in front of them. The Mayfield Theatre Building, with its windows covered by old movie advertisements and its rusted marquee, provided an all too accurate backdrop for the procession. Eliot took a sip of his cappuccino, which tore a fissure in the tulip his barista had poured into the foam. He set the cup upon the counter and used his bottom lip to wipe the residual foam from the stubble growing beneath his nose. A school bus pulled up to the stop sign where only a moment ago a line of classic cars had waited to escort a veteran of life to his designated spot in the cold ground. Eliot watched as a little boy, maybe eight or nine years old and sitting near the back of the bus, scooped a booger from his nose and, after studying it for a long moment, wiped it someplace unseen below the window line as the bus drove away in the same direction as the hearse.

* * *

Eliot tossed his coffee cup into a recycling bin and entered the Cleveland Museum of Art through the North Entrance. His skin burned from the cold whip of the wind against his bare face. The bit of scruff that had accumulated around his jaw line over the past few days did little to shield him from the constant gust funneled along the smooth stone buildings lining either side of East Boulevard. Snow had been piled to the height of Eliot's hip by a sidewalk plow still at work clearing a maze of routes in and out of the museums and administrative offices. Except for the street-crossing, which forced him to climb over two mounds of dappled snow, one to get into the street and another to reach the manicured sidewalk on the other side, he had managed to keep his feet mostly dry until he was inside, where the snow stuck to his jeans began to melt into the tops of his shoes. Shaking the excess snowflakes from his baseball cap, Eliot declared that he had just about had enough of this extended winter, and quickly did the math in his head to count out the number of days until pitchers and catchers would report to Goodyear, Arizona for Spring Training: *Forty-four.*

His eyes slowly adjusted to the dimly lit foyer of the Art Museum. The ceiling hung low, and the rows of senior citizens filing off a set of Anderson Tour buses and into the coat check line fostered in Eliot a small fit of claustrophobia. As was his habit, Eliot had removed his glasses and began wiping the fog from the lenses with the hem of his shirt while still moving persistently forward. The haze of people overlapped, forcing

Eliot to guess his way through the living stream of visitors exiting and entering the cold.

He arrived at the Atrium unscathed, and stopped in the entryway to reaffix his spectacles to his face where they could perform their necessary function. Eliot marveled at the simplicity of Cleveland's Pantheon: a sea of gray granite interrupted only by a small island of indoor grass sprawled beneath a glass ceiling. This is where he came when he was feeling particularly disheartened. Eliot had always found that he used art the same way that others relied upon prayer in their time of need.

And so he found himself staring up through the clear roof, watching white clouds slink across the pale blue sky before realizing what he was actually seeing were piles of snow slowly accumulating on the glass above. He paused for a minute longer to follow the arc of an airplane racing toward the western horizon and Hopkins International Airport. The brief appearance of the sun brightened his face. When the jet disappeared, Eliot continued walking, unsure where he was headed, but intent upon staying the course toward a set of glass doors opposite him. When he arrived, he was asked to produce a ticket to enter the exhibit, *Silks from Islamic Lands, 1250–1900*. Having no ticket, he took a detour up one of the central stairways into the Armory.

He was alone. Like a coin manipulated by a prestidigitator's slight-of-hand, Eliot had ended up far from where he thought he was going. The commotion of the Atrium had, thankfully, not spread to the second floor where cafés and gift shops were replaced by the steel shells worn by long-dead men of the Middle Ages and the jewel-encrusted pistols outfitted with gilded bayonets later brandished by self-proclaimed gentlemen. Eliot paused before the hull of a knight atop his warhorse at the room's center. The knight's death-red plume matched the cloth trimmings of the horse's saffron, spurring Eliot to consider the pageantry of war. He wondered when the museum would begin to display desert-colored Kevlar vests and Winchester rifles.

Eliot spied a low-sitting wooden bench in the corner of the Armory near a glass case arranged with swords of various lengths and shapes. The two-handed models seemed to him particularly unnecessary. He walked to the bench, digging from his back pocket along the way Joseph Kowalski's small paperback copy of *World War One Poetry*. He sat at the far end of the bench, leaving room for anyone who might wander into the hall, and thumbed through the index in search of a specific verse. He slung one leg over the other so that he could rest the spine of his book in the crook of his knee. Eliot traced the page with a scrape of his index finger, and found that what he was looking for laid in wait on page eighty-five. He snapped the worn pages back toward the center of the book, first at large and then at smaller intervals, finally turning one frail page at a time before arriving at the poem.

He read aloud the hazy ink, brazen in his solitude: "Bent double, like old beggars under sacks, knock-kneed, coughing like hags, we cursed through sludge…" His voice wasn't particularly strong or unique, but it echoed off the glass display cases like a preacher's sermon reverberating throughout a great cathedral. Eliot looked up from the book to imagine those pristine suits of armor trudging through muck, smeared and dented from overwork, mud clinging to ornamental fabric—*not so beautiful in their proper context*, he thought. His eyes returned to the clean pulp of the page. He read a few lines silently to himself, then aloud: "Gas! Gas! Quick, boys! – An ecstasy of fumbling, fitting the clumsy helmets just in time…" An attendant walked around the corner and hushed Eliot with a stare before disappearing as quickly as he had appeared.

The fleeting vigor of a life, too brief. There is nothing sweet nor right about dying for one's country. Wilfred Owen's harried scramble to secure a ventilator to his face was not quite reflected in the polished visors hanging from the museum walls. "The old Lie," Eliot breathed, fumbling over the final lines of the poem that Owen had laid down in Latin as if to prove just how long we've been fooling ourselves. It was sad and beautiful, but Eliot could not bring himself to feel the true weight of those words.

He closed Joe's book, and, for a moment, his tearless eyes. The ripe pages fanned a tang of wilted grass and vanilla into his nose. It was an honest smell. The sun had set, extinguishing the natural gleam provided by the Armory's skylights. On either side of the large tapestries hanging from the tall, stone blocks were a series of lanterns glowing Halloween orange. The light seemed to produce shadows rather than illumination, as if they had been placed in order to accentuate the dark spots in the room. Each suit of armor cast a shadow tenfold against the wall, producing a soundless army of darkness.

A church bell tolled from somewhere inside the Museum. The sound echoed through the galleries and Eliot's mind, leaving an abstract impression before it was gone. Thinking that the sound belonged to a timepiece, he patted his pockets for his phone in order to check the hour. When after a second round of interrogation, he hadn't located the device he realized that he had forgotten it in his car.

Eliot exited the Armory by way of the East Wing, following the noise. Walking down a long glass hallway that overlooked the snow-covered rose garden, Eliot spied his car parked against a drift of snow on the opposite side of East Boulevard. At the end of the hall, he turned a sharp corner and entered the gallery of Contemporary Art where the leaden reverberations were still faintly palpable.

Eliot had to squeeze past a group of drawing students from the Institute of Art who were sitting cross-legged on the floor with oversized sketchbooks in their laps and an array of charcoal pencils strewn before them like an elaborate game of Pick-up Stix. He stepped carefully so as not to disturb their focus on the strange wooden sculpture at the center of the room that reminded Eliot of an avocado pit. A number of them looked at him as if he were out of place. He had seen these faces before. Mostly, when he and Nick would claim a seat at Jacob's Field for which they did not have tickets—a phenomenon that would happen quite regularly during the middle innings when they would move from their seats higher up into the vacant plastic thrones of rows *A* through *F*. He had never turned around to look, but he could imagine the glares directed at them were something like the art students' frowns of derision as they marched down the steep concrete steps toward the flawless green of the field. He raised a hand to admit his guilt and softly mouthed *sorry* to the fiercest of scowlers, which seemed to assuage her anger.

Once he had successfully made it through the barricade of knotted limbs and excessive art supplies, Eliot caught his first glimpse of what had made the sound that lured him to the room. Opposite the gigantic avocado pit stood two wobbling iron rods with steel chimes affixed at their tops. A sign had been taped to the floor next to the singing bars that read, "Please ask a security guard to make this sculpture sound." Eliot looked around to see if anyone was present. Approaching him from the back wall near Andy Warhol's *Marilyn Diptych* was a guy about his own age—less scruffy, suited, and wearing a single white glove—who asked if he'd like to hear the "Sonambient." Eliot said that he would and the attendant casually squeezed the two iron bars together allowing their tips to chime. He then wordlessly walked away, pulling the glove from his hand one finger at a time.

Another white-gloved gallery worker, kneeling before a small wicker chair, brushing a week's accumulation of dust from its woven fibers with a soft comb, rubbernecked momentarily as the steel clapped before returning his attention to the job at hand. His gesture reminded Eliot of the conversation he and Alice had with Nick about the Washington Arch near NYU. Alice had asked if New Yorkers eventually got bored with the splendor of the city, if everything kind of became background music, a mere soundtrack to life's banalities. The duster's response to the repeated tolling of the sculpture, a mix of surprise and wonder, elicited from Eliot a sense of doom. Beautiful things, New York things, would remain attractive in the face of routine exposure. Alice was gone.

The high-pitched gong melted away, offering Eliot an opportunity to detect an orchestra of movement: the crinkle of maps folding and unfolding, the timpani of high heeled tourists plodding along wooden floors, and the hushed shuffle of attendants' weary steps echoing against the high ceilings of adjacent galleries. As he turned to retreat from the sculpture Eliot's knees creaked, adding his signature to the arrangement.

It was pleasantly cool in the gallery, and Eliot unbuttoned his heavy jacket to better appreciate the near void of climate, which is when he realized that the room also lacked any smell––the aroma of Joseph Kowalski's book of war poems still lingered in his nose as if trying to remain relevant beyond the Armory. He looked around the room, deciding what to study next. The brilliant colors of a stained-glass arch pulled him to the far corner. Its color and symmetry were violently intense. Standing before it Eliot felt beautifully, wonderfully irrelevant. And then the kaleidoscopic geometry began to take on a familiar shape. The piece was not stained glass, but a *memento mori* composed of household paint and thousands of butterfly carcasses shellacked to canvas. He turned away disgusted by the carnage and walked to the extreme opposite end of the gallery where he paused before a barren depiction of deeply recessed train tracks leading nowhere. Near the bottom, gray and textured with flaked concrete, the artist had scrawled in white chalk *Lot's Fraü*.

Eliot approached the information placard: Anselm Kiefer, *Lot's Wife* (1989); Oil paint, ash, stucco, chalk, linseed oil, polymer emulsion, salt, and applied elements (e.g., copper heating coil) on canvas attached to lead foil on plywood panels. He learned that the painting was based on Kiefer's photos of train tracks in France, and that the raw natural materials and destructive artistic process were meant to symbolize the overwhelming human tragedy of the Holocaust.

Eliot saw, instead, the frozen wasteland of the Collinwood rail yard where he had worked the previous winter installing new electrical boxes that powered the track alignment and turnout mechanisms. In the remote distance of the piece he could make out the gray silhouette of Cleveland's skyline beneath clouds of salt dripping into the negative space of ash and plaster. Small mounds of debris had fallen from the piece onto the hardwood floor over the previous quarter century.

He wasn't sure how long he had been studying the painting before his thoughts turned to his broken engagement with Alice. Nor could he identify what had persuaded his attention to stray—perhaps the itch of his nearly-healed tattoo, or maybe it was Kiefer's untidy lettering that dedicated his painting to Lot's curious bride.

"So, are you going to marry me, or what?" She had asked suddenly as the two of them sat at the bar sharing a plate of roasted root vegetables and drinking Bloody Marys garnished with okra and squash blossoms. It was the second time in as many days that they found themselves quaffing at a vegan café to recover from Thanksgiving festivities at the Browne's three-bedroom Cape Cod on Franklin Street. A series of inquisitive aunts and uncles and cousins had arrived at the house to meet the boy who was stealing Alice away to Cleveland.

Alice had picked up her drink to take a sip, and clanked the salted rim of her glass against his, which seemed to the both of them to perform a pact not dissimilar from the unshakeable bond of a pinky swear. They drank.

"So that's that?" Eliot asked.

"Engaged to be engaged," Alice said and kissed the corner of his mouth.

The sculpture behind Eliot chimed a deeper, more robust sound than it had previously made, drawing his mind back into the present. His head spun around and he saw that a different attendant had crashed the rods together less delicately than the one who manipulated it for him only a few minutes ago. The new attendant, who hadn't bothered to glove his hand, lumbered away with his arms swinging wildly. He disappeared through the doorway leading to a photography exhibit— *America's Haunted Houses*. Eliot followed.

He promptly sat down on a bench across from a massive black and white photograph of the Lemp Mansion in St. Louis, Missouri. He had never heard of the place, but seeing the haunted house made him think of his mother, the other absent woman in his life, in a way that he had never before considered her.

Eliot Hopkins was the result of two people more in love with each other than most would ever be able to understand, let alone experience. His parents were exceptionally paired. Some might call it fated; Frank certainly had on multiple occasions. When Eliot's mother died, the last face she looked upon was not that of her newborn baby, but rather her husband's—twisted between the extremes of joy and sorrow— both, yet neither. Eliot closed his eyes and saw, too, his great-grandparents as they were in the photo taken upon the tree lawn of the house on East 74th Street. They had their struggles, but endured. No matter how many different ways he could imagine his life, that house would always be haunted, and his story would always be a ghost story.

He envisioned the forces that brought Yuri and Muriel together from somewhere across the Atlantic to the rusty shores of Lake Erie. It was something more powerful than religion, and more believable, too. He considered the improbability of Frank and Olivia growing up next door to one another, and the near impossible occurrence of them falling and remaining steadily in love long enough to create a baby, but not a life, together. And he wondered if the magic had run out in the Maternity Ward of St. Vincent Charity Hospital on July 8, 1991, and that tragedy had been in store for him and Alice all along—the inheritors of a used up enchantment.

Eliot was getting tired, and allowing his eyes to rest felt good. The fluorescent lighting in the photo gallery pierced his eyelids, casting a dull crimson glow the color of war's trappings against the intended blackness.

"Hey, man. We're closing up," said the same attendant who had worked the chime for Eliot earlier. He had prematurely unbuttoned his suit coat and loosened his tie. Even his hair seemed more relaxed than before.

"Oh. Yeah. No problem," Eliot said, raising the curtains of his eyes and stammering to his feet. "Um. Hey, thanks for working the chimes earlier. I've never been in this room before."

"The Sonambient," he reminded Eliot. "The artist actually recorded eleven albums during his lifetime. If you're interested, we carry a few of them in the gift shop, which should be open for a few more minutes; they're always happy to pull in some extra dollars at the end of the day. His name is Harry Bertoia."

"Thanks." Eliot had no intention of purchasing the record, but appreciated the attendant's knowledge of the piece. "What's your name?" Eliot asked. It was something he had gotten in the habit of doing after working at the bookstore. It always kind of made his day when a customer would ask him his name and thank him for his help—like he wasn't simply peddling books, but enriching lives.

"Dave."

"Thanks, Dave," he offered his hand in order to shake and Dave took it. "I'm Eliot."

"Right on, Eliot. Check out those albums. And if you're interested, here's my card." He pulled a business card from his wallet and handed it to Eliot. It contained a website and email address underscored by a drawing of a gauntleted fist clutching a sword.

"You write comics?"

"Graphic novels."

"So did my mom," Eliot said, not meaning to share the last bit. He was still looking at the card.

"Really? Anything I'd know?" Dave asked.

Eliot had never seen any of his mother's work; he had only heard about it briefly from his father the afternoon he introduced Frank to Alice. "Probably not. She was a local artist like twenty years ago—children's books mostly.

Dave nodded his understanding.

"Listen, thanks for the card, though. I'll check out your stuff."

"Cool. Well, we had better get out of here. Snow's really coming down now; be careful out there."

* * *

Eliot Hopkins leaned against a tall streetlamp that he and Pat Murphy had installed during a brief thaw that spread across the Great Lakes region from Chicago to Buffalo at the tail end of October. He pulled tight at the scarf knotted around his neck and sunk his hands deep inside his coat's pockets for protection from the midnight wind. The book of war poems was tucked beneath his armpit and pinned close to his body. He had grabbed it instinctively as he left his car in the Belvoir parking lot just beyond the East Gate guard shack, even though he had no real use for it in the blizzard. While he had been standing at the end of the winding walkway leading up to Campion Hall, a route he had passed over many times before on the his way to Alice's room, a layer of snow had completely covered his broad shoulders. His eyes scanned the dormitory windows for signs of life, or afterlife, but saw nothing. The building looked to be vacant. Through the cloud of snowflakes that revealed to him the wind's every gesture, Eliot thought he spotted someone walking toward him from the direction of the Science Center, and hoped that it was Kate.

As the shape approached, he realized that it was a small deer moving from the open-air of the quad to the wooded area behind the football stadium. It carelessly crossed the empty street and disappeared behind the dorm far from where Eliot was waiting. He extended his arm and peeled back the cuff of his coat, exposing the face of his watch to the elements: 12:03am. Before tucking it away, he brushed the few flakes of snow that had settled on the watch's face. It was only December and already the accumulation had begun to weigh on him, the magic had gone out. Eliot's thoughts drifted toward summer, when he would sit in his garage on a lawn chair next to a cooler full of icy beers and listen to Tom Hamilton call the Indians game through the familiar static of AM radio. As the game ended, the sun would sink through the pollution hanging over Detroit, turning the western sky an imperial violet out over the lake. Maybe he would invite Nick down from New York for a week or so just to play catch in the side lot. He would look up, shielding his eyes with his catcher's glove against the glare of the falling sun, to peer into the window that should have been Alice's study on the second floor. No one would sit there punching at the keys of the old

Royal Standard No. 5, creating worlds far more beautiful than the one in which they lived. At least there would be less snow.

A car pulled out from the Belvoir lot with its headlights pointed directly at Eliot so that he couldn't see the make or model until it cut left and rolled to a stop a few inches from the curb. The exaggerated bass of a whitewashed hip-hop anthem rattled the non-descript four-door until the driver punched the mute button and lowered the passenger-side window. She leaned across the seats and asked, "Are you Eliot?"

"Yeah?" Eliot said.

"Kate said to let you know she's on her way. She just had to lock up, then she'd be right over."

"Okay," he said as the window slowly rose and the music kicked back on. The car's wheels spun, then glided a couple of inches before catching enough traction to take off. His exchange with the driver took place so quickly that Eliot wasn't able to discern if she had been one of the two girls he had met at Presti's that afternoon. The silver sedan hung a sliding left at the corner and was gone. The clatter of the factory-grade sound system no longer shook Eliot's clothes, and a serene stillness overtook the landscape. The wind died down, ushering the snow more gently to the ground. As if looking out from beneath a hand-knit blanket, Eliot could see between the heavy snowflakes something tracing the deer tracks across the mostly empty parking lot as it steadily approached.

It took about five minutes from the time he first saw her at the far end of the lot for her to arrive next to him under the streetlamp. "Sorry!" Kate yelled from a few dozen feet away. "A few of us had to stay late to collect data before shutting down."

"Not a problem."

"Thanks," she said and dug around the bottom of her purse for her keys. "I can't find anything in this thing. Here, can you hold this?" she asked, handing him a copy of *The Amazing Adventures of Kavalier & Clay*.

"Hey! Great book," Eliot said.

"I haven't actually started it yet. I picked it up it a few weeks ago and I just haven't had the time to get very far into it." Eliot inspected the book for dog-eared corners, and found that page 339 had been folded in upon itself, indicating that it was the copy he had given to Alice after he had suggested they dress up as The Escapist and Luna Moth for their first Halloween together. Eliot hadn't celebrated the holiday in a long time, but Alice really wanted to put together a couple's costume, and he couldn't bring himself to say no.

"Oh, man, it sings! You'll love them," Eliot assured her.

Kate looked up. "Them?" She asked, studying his face for a prolonged second.

"Joe Kavalier and Sam Clay. The book. You'll dig it."

Brandishing her keys she asked, "Are you coming?"

Eliot nodded and handed her back his book, which she dropped into the abyss of her handbag. The two of them ascended the heavily salted walkway toward Campion Hall, Kate leading the way. Before they entered the vestibule Eliot turned to take a last look at the steadily falling snow. And then they were indoors. The hum of the vending machines filled the vacant space. It was dark in every direction.

Kate reiterated that she was pretty sure that she was the only student currently staying in Campion, but that from time to time a hallway light had been switched on—maybe it was a janitor, she guessed. Eliot felt suddenly trapped.

He stopped at the elevator and pressed the call button as he was used to riding up to the third floor with Alice—more out of convenience than laziness. Her room was only a few doors away from the lift, but at the opposite end of the hall from the stairwell.

"They shut off the power to the elevators during break," Kate said. "We're taking the stairs." She continued down the narrow hallway without pause, her shoes leaving wet footprints upon the tiles. Eliot followed. Doors decorated with dry erase boards, scantily clad pictures of the room's inhabitants, and small pieces of John Carroll paraphernalia that had no doubt been purchased by proud parents for exorbitant amounts of money at the campus bookstore ran the entire length of the hall. In all the times he had been to Alice's room, he had never traversed this strange avenue.

Kate swung open the door to the stairwell and he followed her along the detoured route as she moved deliberately up the steps, like a deer wading through knee-high snow. He cast an embarrassed look down at his feet once he realized that he'd been hypnotized by Kate's shifting hips, swaying before him at eye level as she climbed. Kate looked back at him when they reached the second-floor landing to make sure he continued following her up the stairs, and Eliot imagined Alice giving some poet she hardly knew the same look as they climbed the stairs to her Manhattan apartment after a night of drinking in an NYU bar. He wanted to stop himself, to turn around and go home, as if his act could somehow influence the imagined stranger out of Alice's bed. But when they arrived at the third floor Kate held the door open for him, ushering him into another hallway, almost identical to the one two floors below.

Eliot now walked in front, shepherded toward Alice's door from the opposite direction. Seeing it void of any clues that she had once lived there, the bare wood seemed to him completely foreign. Kate brushed past him and wordlessly slid her key into the lock, then used her hip to push the door open into the room.

Once inside, Eliot could see that everything had been changed. When he and Alice had spent long evenings watching assigned films for her class the room had been divided neatly down the middle: a bed and desk pushed to the extreme of each wall had left room for a loveseat beneath the window overlooking South Belvoir. Kate had rearranged so that now both desks were pushed together beneath the window and the beds were stacked into bunks. The couch pressed against the opposite wall where, once, Alice had slept. Kate elected to keep the overhead light turned off, and instead knelt down at the foot of her bed to plug in an extension cord that powered a set of purple Christmas lights she had strung up around the ceiling.

Kate shook off her coat and threw it over the back of the desk chair. Eliot waited as Kate turned on her computer's speakers and a hypnotic love song. He left his coat on, fully expecting to gather his few belongings and leave for home.

The haunting chant of song coupled with the violet glow of imagined summer evenings urged him further into Kate's foreign world.

Like Po'Sam holding court with a Fender Stratocaster atop the stone steps of the Cain Park Amphitheater, Kate was undeniable. Eliot could only watch as the scene unfolded; he had become a mere actor in her production, directed by the motion of her body perfectly synced with the background hymn. Her hand teased at the buttons of her blouse while her eyes studied Eliot for the slightest reaction. His mind was addled, unsure of how to stop what was certainly about to happen, and unsure, too, if he wanted it to stop. Kate extended her hand and placed the tips of her fingers against his chest, easing him toward the couch. His heel clipped a corner of the lidless plastic bin he had come to retrieve from the room, sending his full weight toppling into the plush of the couch. A jar of melted snow rolled across the floor. Eliot tried to seize the moment of clarity offered by this distraction, but Kate stood before him unbuttoning her jeans—he knew that this had been planned; and he knew that he was fucked.

Dissolution
December 31, 2013

ELIOT MUST HAVE FALLEN asleep because when he opened his eyes Kate was gone. The small heap of her clothes lay unmoved next to the couch; his own garments were strewn less neatly about the floor. "I'm going to take a shower," he remembered her saying, though he wasn't certain how long ago that had been, or how long she planned on being gone—something he would know from experience if it were Alice. The moment this thought entered his mind (the average duration of an Alice Browne shower) he felt the inescapable weight of regret that would remain with him for the rest of his life. He was certain of the remorse he had waiting for him. That was all he had.

Eliot felt like the lonely man in James Dean's "Ode to a Tijuana Toilet" who can't get out from the back of the mirror. His gaze was fixed on the blank, white ceiling, trying to work his way backwards to figure out how he had gotten here. The warmth of the room and the lingering smell of sex made it impossible to think. He suddenly had an urge to get high. The sweet, familiar cloud of burning marijuana might give him an excuse other than she was there and beautiful and he was weak. Eliot reached out an arm to search his coat pockets for a joint that he knew wasn't there.

He rustled through the pockets one by one, eventually coming up empty handed. The coat finally slid to the floor from its place atop the plastic bin, uncovering his great-grandfather's baseball cap and a manila folder filled with a neatly aligned stack of paper. A pair of crisscrossing rubber bands secured the sheaf at its center like a decorative ribbon used to adorn a carefully wrapped gift. He lifted the bundle half hoping it contained instructions for recovering lost integrity, and removed the first rubber band and then the second with the same reckless impatience he had displayed while undressing Kate. He opened the folder and read the two short lines in the middle of an otherwise blank page: *Fall Classics, A Novel by Alice Browne.*

Eliot closed the folder as if to hide his guilt from the name printed upon those pages. *She had left it because she knew he would come to retrieve his things.* He thought about getting dressed and leaving the room before Kate returned. By the time he reached his car in the parking lot across the street, he might have convinced himself that the whole ordeal had never occurred, and that he and Alice could salvage the ruin of their relationship through the same long-distance miracle that had united Yuri and Muriel.

But he was possessed—no more able to move from the purgatory of that couch than any fictional character is able to escape from the ink stains of their printed sins. He thought of Jay Gatsby and Daisy Buchanan, of Sal Paradise and Dean Moriarty, and now, too, of Eliot Hopkins and Kate—whose last name he did not know.

As was the custom when he was feeling particularly ashamed, Eliot considered his mother who had died bringing him into the world, and his father who had taught him to be unfailingly selfless. He was their legacy: the heartbreaking conclusion to an otherwise charmed story that began with his great-grandparents in the trenches of a frozen coal-mining town in Minnesota while the world was at war, and which blossomed mightily on the shores of Lake Erie.

Eliot opened the folder resting in his lap. Flipping past the title page of Alice Browne's novel, he faced his penance. Eliot read slowly, weighing his remorse against the grace of her words. At the end of the first paragraph he set her pages aside, closed his eyes, and wept.

Acknowledgements

My gratitude to the Vassar College English Department, the Dean of the Faculty Office, and The Tatlock Endowed Fund for supporting this work. Research for this novel was undertaken at the Thompson Memorial Library at Vassar College, The Cleveland Museum of Art, The Western Reserve Historical Society, and Lake View Cemetery. While I drew upon and included many details from the rich history of Cleveland, I changed a bunch of stuff, too.

I am indebted foremost to Nicholas Pauley for asking me to advise his senior independent study: 'Fiction and Empathic Consciousness.' The course offered us an opportunity to consider the merits of fiction writing as a viable critical mode—one that gives us a complex view of isolation and empathy in contemporary American literature, society, and politics. Nick's final project took the form of a drafted novel. To better understand the process he was going through, I elected to write alongside him. Such was the impetus for *On Coventry*. Over the course of an academic year we shared with one another a handful of pages per week. Nick's generosity with his time was trumped only by the thoughtfulness of his feedback.

Every writer has in mind an ideal reader, one who will be meticulous, critical, and supportive. Since I met him in 2006, that reader has been Joe Webb. We were colleagues in the doctoral program in English literature at Saint Louis University, and Joe was an infinitely better writer than I was at the time. He charitably read all my stuff, and offered me a remarkable amount of attention. He was, and continues to be, a superlative motivator and superior teacher. I'm most pleased, however, to call him one of my dearest friends. Thanks for everything, buddy.

A great many thanks to Adam LaSota, who introduced me to Cleveland punk rock, college radio, and junkyards—all of which require a degree of elbow grease and know-how inherited from previous generations. To Tim Snider, the most loyal Clevelander I know. Tim taught me that rooting for a sports team is no small thing, and that traversing a place one mile at a time is how you really get to know it. We cruised the city across numerous summers on the back of a couple 750cc motorcycles, inviting Cleveland and its environs to become an inseparable part of us.

My deepest respect and gratitude to my parents, Brian and Carol, for instilling in me a work ethic that reflects everything good and mighty about the Midwest. They gave everything so that their children could follow their dreams. I hope the fact that we did makes all the sacrifices worth it. To my brother, Brad, who is the best of men: unfailingly generous, infinitely compassionate. He is an inspiration to live a happy life.

This is a work of fiction. And though it is Eliot's story, his life is full of talented and beautiful women. Some are painfully absent, others painfully present. My wife Jayme, a constant presence—ethical, winsome, Clevelander!—deserves an enormous amount of praise for supporting me through the process of writing this book even as she was pregnant with our son, Arthur. She outshines everyone who lives in these pages. It is my hope that this story conveys our mutual admiration and love for Northeast Ohio.

About the Author

Matthew Schultz was born in Cleveland, Ohio. He holds a B.A. and M.A. in English literature from John Carroll University and a Ph.D. in modern Irish literature from Saint Louis University. He is the author of *Haunted Historiographies: The Rhetoric of Ideology in Postcolonial Irish Fiction*. He lives in New York, and teaches at Vassar College. This is his first novel.

More books from
Harvard Square Editions: